JOHN WILSON

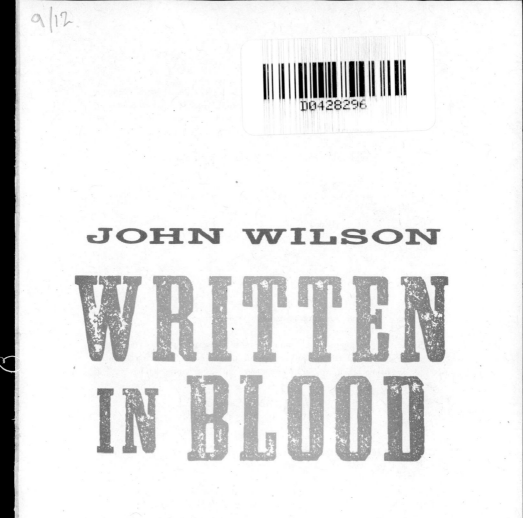

WRITTEN IN BLOOD

ORCA BOOK PUBLISHERS

Library and Archives Canada Cataloguing in Publication

Wilson, John (John Alexander), 1951-
Written in blood / written by John Wilson.

Issued also in an electronic format.
ISBN 978-1-55469-270-5

I. Title.
PS8595.I5834W75 2010   jC813'.54   C2010-903600-X

First published in the United States, 2010
Library of Congress Control Number: 2010929062

Summary: A young man's search for the father who abandoned him takes him
through the wilds of the Arizona Territory and northern Mexico during the 1870s
and brings him in contact with an assortment of intriguing characters.

Mixed Sources
Cert no. SW-COC-001271
© 1996 FSC
FSC

*Orca Book Publishers is dedicated to preserving the environment and has printed this book
on paper certified by the Forest Stewardship Council.*

Orca Book Publishers gratefully acknowledges the support for its publishing programs
provided by the following agencies: the Government of Canada through the Canada Book
Fund and the Canada Council for the Arts, and the Province of British Columbia through
the BC Arts Council and the Book Publishing Tax Credit.

Cover and text design by Teresa Bubela
Typesetting by Nadja Penaluna
Cover photo by Getty Images
Author photo by Katherine Gordon

ORCA BOOK PUBLISHERS
PO Box 5626, Stn. B
Victoria, BC Canada
V8R 6S4

ORCA BOOK PUBLISHERS
PO Box 468
Custer, WA USA
98240-0468

www.orcabook.com
Printed and bound in Canada.

13 12 11 10 • 4 3 2 1

*For Rick and Anita, with thanks for
the home-away-from-home.*

This is a world whose history is written in blood. Blood drenches the black dried scabs of the rocks, the rusty desert sands and the distant crimson mountains bathed in the dying light of the setting sun. It is the blood that has drained from conquistadores, Apaches, Mexicans, Americans, leaving their empty bodies to dry out in the unforgiving sun. Not for the first time, I wonder what the hell I'm doing here on this fool's errand.

I am camped on the edge of an eroded bluff of black volcanic rock. The only sounds are the quiet chomping of my tethered horse eating the nearby clumps of grass sprouting from cracks in the rock and the sizzle of the skinned jackrabbit on the stick over the crackling fire in front of me. The sky above is the deepest black I have ever seen and the stars so bright and close I feel I could reach out and pluck them.

I stare over my fire to the west, across the desert plain I crossed today, at the barely discernable black outline of the mountains where I camped last night. The tiny flickering campfire out on the plain is the only light. Every night for the past five days I have seen this fire as darkness falls. There is probably a man sitting by it looking up at the light of my fire. Who is he? Perhaps he is simply a traveler, taking the same route as I, but the loneliness of this place makes me think not. What his purpose is, I cannot guess. All I know is that every evening his campfire is a little closer.

I chose this place to camp because these low hills command a view of the way I have come, because there are some stunted trees for shelter should the clouds I saw building at twilight turn into a storm, and because there is a nearby spring for fresh water. It's a good spot, but it's not the land I have left.

Three months ago, on my sixteenth birthday, I was leaning on the rail of the schooner *Robert Boswell*, watching porpoises leap around us as we tacked across the Strait of Georgia toward the Strait of Juan de Fuca and the Pacific Ocean. My world then was blue—the dark blue of the water below, the pale blue of the sky above and blue-gray of the mountains at my back. I have not seen blue since I stepped off the ship in San Diego and launched myself into this land of rusty brown, burnt ocher and blood. The eternal snow on the peaks of the mountains back home is merely the memory of a dream.

My thoughts drift back to the modest parlor of the stopping house in Yale that my parents built in 1859 with gold my father had clawed from the Fraser River. I was born two years later, by which time business was booming as thousands of hopeful miners flooded through Yale on their way to the goldfields of the Cariboo, nursing their dreams of untold wealth.

I remember my mother telling me, "Your father found gold in the Fraser River, but we made a lot more money from the fools going to look for gold in the Cariboo."

My father came up from California to look for gold in the District of New Caledonia in May of '58. By the time New Caledonia became British Columbia later that year, he had staked and was working three good claims near Yale. Before a year was out, he had sold them, met and married my mother and bought the lot where our stopping house was to stand. But my father was not a man to let the grass grow beneath his feet. By the time British Columbia became the sixth province of Canada in 1871, he had been gone for four years.

I don't think my mother even resented my father leaving. I suspect she had known since they first laid eyes on each other that he would move on one day. He had what my mother called an impatient soul.

"Some folks just can't settle down in one place," she used to say. "They aren't made that way. With people like that you've got two choices: give up everything and accompany them, or accept that one day they'll be gone and enjoy the time that you are in the same place with them.

"Your father gave me two very precious things when he left me the stopping house: financial security and independence. Both of them are great rarities for women, and I wasn't about to give them up easily. And then there was you. I knew you'd leave one day too. I saw your father's restless spirit in your eyes the day you were born, but even a rambler needs roots and a strong foundation. I stayed and ran the stopping house to give you that."

On the last day before I left, my mother and I stood on opposite sides of the polished oak table in the parlor. She looked sad but not angry or tearful.

"Well, James, if you're heart-set on going, all I can do is wish you luck and give you this." She handed me a tin box that I knew well. I set it on the table, undid the latch and lifted the lid. Inside, Dad's Colt Pocket revolver lay nestled in a bed of worn red felt. Beside it was a powder horn, a bullet mold, a box of percussion caps and a collection of lead bullets. It's an old gun; you have to load each of the six chambers individually with powder, shot and percussion cap; but my father always said that was no disadvantage over the new fancy revolvers that took the ready-made cartridges.

"A handgun's only good for shooting at something closer than a hundred feet away," he used to say. "If you're that close to a man and you need more than one or two shots, you're probably already dead."

I practiced with the revolver until I became a pretty good shot, and I feel comfortable knowing that it's lying with my saddlebags across the fire from me.

"Won't you need it once I'm gone?" I asked my mother when she gave me the gun.

"No use for a gun here now," she said with a smile. "This is 1877. When your father first came up here, it was a different matter. There were a lot of rough characters coming through then and not much law to control them, but all that's changed. We've got laws and government now. A lady doesn't have need of a handgun here, but you may where you're going."

"I have to go and find out what happened to Dad," I said. "I always said I would as soon as I was old enough and able. I'll be sixteen in three days and I've got some money saved, so there's no point in waiting."

Mother nodded slowly. "When you make up your mind, nothing changes it. You're stubborn, just like him. He kept his thoughts close to himself, but once his mind was made up, God Almighty himself couldn't change it. I know I can't stop you going but, remember, you may not find him. He told me he was going to Mexico, but Mexico's a big place. Besides, he may not wish to be found or," she hesitated, "something may have happened to him."

"That's true, but somewhere down there, someone knows where he is or what happened to him, and I aim to find that out."

"Even if you find him," mother said thoughtfully, "he may not be what you expect. You were only six years old when he left, and he'll be forty-five by now. What do you remember about him?"

"I can see him like it was yesterday, not tall but strong. He could lift me like I was a feather. His hair was dark, but I was always fascinated by how red it was at the ends, especially his mustache where it dropped down the sides of his mouth. When I was little, I always thought he grew that mustache to try and pull down the edges of the smile he always wore.

"I remember him teaching me Spanish and telling me stories. He told me about the *vaqueros* and Spanish grandees in Mexico, the wild Apache Indians and cowboys in Arizona and New Mexico, and the gold prospectors and gamblers in California. I promised myself that I would go and see these places for myself one day."

"He was a good storyteller," mother said wistfully. "But there was a lot about his life before I met him that he never did tell, and God knows I asked often enough. For all his talk and tales, he was a secretive man, never wanted anyone to really know him. I wondered sometimes if he had something dark in his past that he was running from. He used to have nightmares, you know. I'd wake to find him sitting in the bed beside me, bathed in sweat, his eyes wide and staring as if the room was full of ghosts. I used to ask what he saw in the night, but he never told me. Always passed it off as something he ate for supper that disagreed with him."

"I didn't know."

"No reason for you to know. Mostly they were in the years after I first met him. They eased off after we got the stopping house set up and running, but they came back in the months before he left. I guess what I'm trying to say is that there was more to your father than the stories he told. You might be disappointed when you meet him."

I opened my mouth to protest, but Mother went on. "I'm not trying to talk you out of going. I know you've got his obsessions, and nothing I can say will change that. I just want you to go down there with your eyes open, because, even if all his stories were true, things have changed. It's not the world he knew down there twenty years ago. There are cattlemen, cowboys and gunfighters moving in there now. Civilization's creeping in, but it's a slow, violent process."

"But I have to try," I repeated.

"I know, and I've tried to give you the best tools I can. You're a fair shot with that revolver, you can at least stay on the back of a horse, and I've encouraged you to keep up with the Spanish he taught you. I also hope I've given you the sense to know when to stand and fight and when to run. So I guess all that's left is to wish you luck."

We embraced, and the next morning at daybreak I was gone to New Westminster to catch the *Robert Boswell*.

So I am down here in the desert to search for a father I have not seen in ten years, but my quest is not as futile as it may seem, or as my mother thinks. I have a clue, a starting point that she gave me and yet knows nothing of.

As soon as Mother thought I was old enough, she began teaching me how to use father's revolver. I treasured it and spent long hours practicing loading, shooting and cleaning it. One day, after I had been in the woods at target practice, I was cleaning the gun in my room when I dropped the box, and the felt lining where the revolver nestled came loose. Beneath it was a letter my father had written before he left and which he had obviously intended me to find one day. I have it in my jacket pocket now, but I do not need to take it out. I know every word by heart.

Dear James,

I do not know when, or even if, you will find this, but I hope you will read it one day.

I also sincerely wish that you do not hold a grudge against me for leaving, but, as I hope you will one day understand, I had little choice.

I know how much you love sitting by my knee listening to the stories of my life in Mexico and California, and those occasions were a great joy to me also, but you must know that I changed the stories for the ears of a six-year-old boy and that there are things that I left out, things that not even your mother knows.

For all the stories I told, I said nothing of my family or early life. It is not that I am ashamed, but it was a difficult, complex time that I wanted to leave behind when I came north and met your mother. I planned to tell you everything one day when you'd be old enough to understand, and perhaps one day we may still have the opportunity to set the record straight, but the fact that you're reading this letter suggests that I may not have that chance.

I do not wish to go into details in this letter, suffice it to say that in journeying north, I had managed to leave the past behind. Marrying your mother and your arrival are the two most important things I have done, and my time in Yale with you both was the happiest of my life.

Unfortunately, I was mistaken in thinking that it is possible to escape one's past; you take it with you wherever you go. Things have occurred recently that make my departure, if I wish to protect your mother and you, essential.

I have told your mother nothing of all this as I am certain she would insist on trying to help me and that is not possible. She believes that I am moving on in response to my restless soul, and I would ask that you not disabuse her of this idea.

I will journey to Don Alfonso Ramirez's hacienda outside Casas Grandes in Chihuahua State in Mexico, and there attempt to resolve these difficulties. If I am successful, I shall return to you swiftly. If I have not come back, it is because I continue to try or have perished in the attempt.

I do not relish leaving, but you and your mother are well provided for. She is a strong and resourceful woman, and you show signs already of growing into an intelligent and quick-witted boy. I take comfort from knowing that the pair of you will prosper. Perhaps one day, when you are grown up, we shall meet and I can tell you the full story.

Grow strong and look after your mother.

Believe that I always loved and cared for you and your mother and that I always will.

Your father,

Bob Doolen

I never blamed my father for leaving, and I never did tell my mother about the letter. It was a secret between my father and me, and the more I read the letter, the more I began to believe that he had written it to give me clues that would start me on a journey to discover the story that, for some reason, he couldn't tell me. I swore to myself that, as soon as I was able, I would seek out my father and learn the truth. I would start by finding Don Alfonso Ramirez at Casas Grandes in Chihuahua.

One year ago, I sent a letter to Señor Ramirez, but I received no reply. I don't know what this means; the letter may have gotten lost or Señor Ramirez may have moved away or died. Two months ago, I sent a second letter outlining my plans to come down. Again I received no reply, but who knows? Perhaps someone read the letter and awaits my arrival. One way or another, I intend to follow the trail that my father left.

In San Diego I purchased my pony and tack from a Mexican who had ridden her all the way from Texas and was about to take passage down the coast to Acapulco. I suspect I paid above the going rate for her. She is not a pretty animal, being a dirty dun color and small, but she is good-natured, hardy and used to the desert. And she and I have become friends. She is my only companion and I talk to her. I tell stories of life in Yale and of my father and why I am here. Her name is Alita, after a girl who fought in the battles that made Mexico free from Spain.

I bartered my carpetbag for a bedroll that straps behind Alita's saddle and bought a pair of saddlebags, a large water canteen and a flint to start fires. I also acquired clothes more suited to desert travel than the ones I brought with me—a wide-brimmed hat, loose shirt and pants, and a woolen jacket and extra blanket, as it is December and the nights on the trail can be bitter.

For food I took flour—with which I have learned to make *tortillas*, a kind of flatbread that people here eat with everything—dried beans, meat and coffee. I have had no trouble replenishing these basic commodities as I travel. Whenever I can, I also carry a bag of grain for Alita, but she is very good at foraging when we stop in the evenings.

In the weeks of my traveling east, I have toughened and discovered much. For the first days, Alita and I progressed at a steady walk. She became restless and I ached as if run over by a herd of stampeding cattle. Now I have learned to vary the pace, sometimes walking, sometimes trotting and sometimes cantering and resting often, and we are both much happier. Through watching and talking with travelers I meet on the trail, I have ascertained something of the habits of the creatures that live hereabouts, enough at any rate to snare some fresh meat on occasion. I am also getting better at reading the land, spotting the places where the trail is easiest and the gullies, *arroyos* they are called here, most likely to carry a stream for fresh water. And I have a book, which I read in spare moments and from which I am attempting to improve the Spanish that my father taught me.

After the first day or two inland from the coast, the land becomes rough and harsh. It is almost as if the earth is wrinkled like old skin into mountains and valleys that run north and south so that the trail is an endless repetition of crossing wide, dry plains and winding through rugged mountain passes. Rain comes in violent evening storms that can turn a dry arroyo into a raging river in minutes. All this is so different from the wet lushness of home. I miss seeing decent-sized trees.

As the jackrabbit sizzles before me, I squint at the campfire only two or three miles away. If the man were stalking me with the intent to rob or murder me, surely he would not let me see his campfire every evening. I find myself almost eager for him to catch up. Alita is a fine companion, but it has been a lonely journey, and, even with my determination and the pride I feel at my good progress, I do miss my mother and my previous life.

Six days ago I crossed the Colorado River on the new bridge at Yuma and headed into Arizona Territory. This time tomorrow I should be in Tucson, and from there I shall confirm my best route to Casas Grandes.

I reach forward and lift the jackrabbit from above the fire. It cools quickly in the evening air, and soon I am pulling the flesh off with my teeth. It's a scrawny beast and it has a bitter taste that I don't recognize from the similar creatures fed on the exuberant vegetation of British Columbia.

I suck the last of the rabbit bones clean, build up the fire, wrap myself in my blanket and settle down.

Is the follower settling down as well? In the distance I hear a coyote bark. Lightning flashes harshly and thunder rumbles to the west. I wonder if I'm going to have a wet night, but I'm asleep before I can think too much about it.

Someone or something is watching me. I can't see them, but I can feel their eyes boring into my back. It's almost fully light and I am lying staring over the dead ashes of the fire. What if it's a wolf? I'll never be able to rise, cross the fire and retrieve and load my revolver before the beast is on me, ripping out my throat. With my heart racing, I roll over.

The man is squatting with his back to a tree, looking at me. For a gut-wrenching moment, I think it's my father. The man is middle-aged and has a drooping mustache, but his skin is too swarthy and he doesn't have my father's smile.

The stranger is dressed in worn traveling clothes and wears a battered wide-brimmed hat. His hair is long and straggles over his ears. His eyes, peering out from under bushy eyebrows, appear almost black. His skin has the weather-beaten look of someone who spends his life in the open. He carries a large Colt Navy revolver tucked into his belt.

"Howdy," the man says. It's an American expression, but the accent has a hint of Spanish.

"Good morning," I reply.

"Didn't want to startle you awake," he says with a slight smile. "You never know who's carrying a pistol beneath their blanket and who ain't afraid to use it afore they think."

"Have you been following me?" I ask, sitting up.

"Following you? Naw. Reckon we're just headed in the same direction and I'm moving a touch faster than you."

"Where are you headed?"

"Tucson," the man replies. "After that, who knows? I hear there's work over in Lincoln County in New Mexico Territory, and a fella can always find something to fill his belly down around Casas Grandes."

"Casas Grandes?" I try to hide my surprise. "You know Casas Grandes?"

The man stares hard at me for a long moment.

"Sure," he says eventually, "everyone hereabouts does. Some big ranching spreads down that way. It's harsh country, so they're always looking for good hands. Trouble is the pay's no good. Probably better off in Lincoln County."

The man stands up, steps forward and holds out his hand.

"Name's Eduardo, but most folks just call me Ed."

"I'm James. Most people call me Jim. Are you Mexican?"

A shadow passes over Ed's face, but then he smiles and goes on.

"I am but I don't make much of it. Ain't no percentage in being Mexican these days. I spent a lot of years up in New Mexico Territory, learned the lingo and the cattle business. If I talk 'merican, folks assume I ain't no Mexican." Ed exaggerates his accent to sound like a rough cowboy. "But when I dine with the grandees in Mexico"—almost magically, Ed's voice becomes soft and cultured with a stronger Spanish accent—"I throw off the coarse smell of cattle and become one of them."

Ed smiles and reverts to, what I assume, is his normal voice. "Anyways, I reckon it's no more'n twenty miles to Tucson, and that's but an easy day's ride, even with your late sleep and on that pony you have." Ed nods to where Alita stands placidly. "What say we keep company? A journey shared is a journey lessened, I always say."

The man tilts his head and gazes at me. He's friendly enough, but there's something about his look that I instinctively don't trust. I'll keep a close watch on him.

"I'd be happy to ride to Tucson with you," I say.

"You ain't from these parts?" Ed asks as we ride, side by side, across a dry plain studded with tall, slender cactus. The sun is up and the air is warming. The thunderclouds of last night have vanished. No rain fell on me, but I can smell dampness in the air and Alita's delicate footsteps kick up no dust.

Ed rides a black gelding considerably larger than Alita, and I have to look up slightly as we talk.

"No. I'm from up north, the colony of British Columbia."

"So you're a Brit then."

"Half," I reply. "My father was an American who came up for the Gold Rush."

"Did he come from these parts?"

"He came up on a ship from California, but he told stories about Mexico, so he knew this area well."

Ed nods. "He still up there in British Columbia?"

"He left my mother and me ten years ago. I haven't seen him since. That's why I came down here, to look for him."

Ed stares over at me thoughtfully as we ride and talk.

"Down here's a big place. How do you aim to find him?"

"His name's Bob Doolen, and he had some connection with the town you mentioned, Casas Grandes. That's where I'll begin."

"Not much to go on," Ed muses, looking ahead to the rough hills on the horizon. "Doolen's an Irish name."

"I guess so. My father never said whether his father was Irish or not."

We lapse into silence and ride on through the morning and I have a chance to examine my companion out of the corner of my eye. He rides comfortably on a worn saddle that shows the remnants of some ornate silver work on the horn. It must once have been worth a lot of money. His bedroll is tied behind the saddle, and two stained and worn saddlebags hang down.

A multicolored Indian blanket sits beneath the saddle and the stock of a large rifle sticks out of a scabbard strapped along the horse's flank. There's something black and stringy hanging from the saddle horn.

In the early afternoon we stop to rest the horses in a small stand of mesquite trees. A heavy thundershower passed over here in the night, and there are pools of water standing in hollows in the red rock. The horses drink and we fill our water bottles. I eat the last of some tortillas and beans I bought two days back, and Ed chews on a long strip of tough-looking jerked meat. I notice that he has the black object from his saddle beside him. He sees me looking at it.

"This is my good luck charm," he says, tossing the thing over to me. "What d'you reckon it is?"

It's an old, irregular piece of dark brown leather from some animal, and there is long black hair hanging from it.

"Piece of bearskin?" I guess.

Ed laughs loudly.

"Reckon you led a sheltered life up yonder in British Columbia. What you're holding there is a genuine human scalp."

I almost drop the grisly relic and hurriedly toss it back up to my companion.

Ed catches it deftly and strokes the hair.

"This here scalp was fresh in 1850, the year I turned sixteen. Scalps were worth good money in them days, a hundred silver dollars for an Apache warrior, fifty for a woman and twenty-five for a child. In some places rate went as high as two hundred and fifty dollars for a warrior scalp."

"That's horrible. Who would offer money for a scalp?"

"Mexican state governments. They put a bounty on Apache scalps, *Ley Quinto* it were called. Still a law down there in many places but not the trade there used to be. Not enough Apaches left and those that are left are hard to catch. Course, it's difficult to tell from a piece of skin and hair if it come from an Apache or a Mexican, so I do hear tell that there's some money to be made still, especially when an Apache band breaks out of the reservation, like Victorio did this past summer up at San Carlos. That scares a lot of good folks, and everyone gets kind of skittish then and is prepared to believe that every old piece of hair is the scalp of one more vicious Apache brave they don't have to worry about."

I sit in shocked silence, listening to Ed's brutal tale. I wonder vaguely why, if scalps were worth so much money, he hadn't sold this one, but I'm not about to ask. Ed goes on talking. He seems to take pleasure in the grim details of the business.

"Around 1850 it were so profitable they had to tighten up the laws. You see, when a scalp's still fresh, it's possible to stretch it. Then you can cut it up into seven or eight pieces, dry them and collect the bounty on each piece. Law said a scalp had to include at least one ear and the crown of the hair.

"Gangs of men made a good living harvesting scalps and didn't pay too much attention to where they came from. One of the best was led by a fella called Roberto Ramirez."

I started at the name from my father's letter, but it was probably a common Mexican surname.

"He weren't no more'n a kid back then, not much older than you are now, I would guess, but he was brutal." Ed looks down at me with an odd, almost conspiratorial smile. "It's said that in one raid in the spring of 1851 Ramirez and his boys took two hundred and fifty scalps in a single day.

"The Ramirez gang had their own way of doing things. Once the shooting was over, each man would take out his scalping knife. He'd sit by the head, run the knife around the scalp, put his feet on the shoulders and pull. Scalp came off as clean as anything—made kind of a popping sound I hear tell. Then all you had to do was sprinkle some salt on it and hang it to dry."

"How do you know all of this?" I ask.

"I been around," Ed says noncommittally, "and those days ain't completely over. I heard it said that Victorio and his band is raiding around the Black Mountain in New Mexico. Nana and Geronimo are still out there raiding in Mexico and Texas. I daresay you could find someone to pay a penny or two for any one of their scalps."

Ed's smile is almost a leer now.

"But enough storytelling. The next range of hills"— he waves a hand at the low rocky ridge that lies about two hour's ride to the east—"is the last one afore Tucson."

We mount up and ride on in silence. I don't feel inclined to encourage Ed to tell me any more stories about scalps or raiding Apaches, and I find myself looking around nervously as we enter the narrow rocky pass through the hills.

Toward the top of the pass, the trail narrows so much that we have to ride in single file, and Ed drops behind me. As we near the top, two riders crest the ridge and descend toward us. They make no attempt to quit the trail and let us past. In fact, they stand their horses abreast at a slightly wider spot in the path and await our arrival.

I rein in a few feet in front of them. Both are filthy from long days on the trail. One is bareheaded and has striking red hair. He is riding a pale pony with a darker mane and tail. The other is no older than I am and wears a battered pork pie hat. His horse is skinny and wild-looking and has a star-shaped white mark on its forehead. Both stare sullenly at me.

"Good day," I say. "May we pass?" Alita shifts restlessly beneath me.

The man with the red hair laughs coarsely, exposing a mouthful of rotting teeth. I swivel in the saddle to see if Ed has any suggestions on how to resolve this. He is sitting, casually holding his Colt Navy above his horse's head. At first I think he is threatening the men, but the revolver is pointing directly at me.

"What?" I ask in confusion.

"Git down," one of the men on the trail orders.

I turn back. Alita is moving backward, away from the strangers, but Ed is crowding us from behind.

"Git down," the redhead repeats. He's pointing an old flintlock rifle with a hexagonal barrel. "I ain't aimin' to ask again."

"Best do as Red asks," Ed says from behind me. "We don't want no unpleasantness."

I hesitate. What's going on? Ed is obviously in on the ambush. Was it planned long ago? Was that why he followed me and joined me on the trail?

As I try to come to terms with what is happening, the kid in the hat swings off his horse and comes forward. He clears his throat noisily and spits before reaching up, grabbing my belt and hauling me unceremoniously out of the saddle.

I fall heavily and a sharp rock sends arrows of pain through my right shoulder. The kid kicks me savagely in the side, and I cry out. I scrabble to one side and look up. In almost unbelievable slow motion the kid pulls a worn revolver from his belt, leans forward and points it between my eyes. The black hole of the barrel seems like a vast bottomless cave, and the sound of the hammer being cocked is deafening.

I'm going to die. I should plead for my life, grab at the revolver, roll to one side, run away. All these things fly through my mind but they are no use; I'm paralyzed and struck dumb by the image of the bullet exploding its way through my skull.

"Hold there, Kid!" Ed's voice is authoritative, but the revolver doesn't move. I can feel the tickle of warm blood running down my arm from where I landed on the rock.

"What d'you mean?" The Kid asks without taking his eyes off me. They are blue and cold. "We allays kill 'em."

"I mean, hold. We ain't gonna kill this one."

I almost cry with relief, but the gun's still pointing at me.

"Ain't gonna kill him? You bin out in the sun too long. That's crazy talk. If'n we don't kill him, he'll have the law on us afore we're half a day's ride away."

"We've outrun the law before, and I say we ain't gonna kill him. Besides, this boy ain't gonna cause trouble. Soon as we're done, he'll be heading back west to California to find a ship home. Ain't that right?"

With an extraordinary effort of will, I look away from the gun muzzle and back over my shoulder at Ed. He's still sitting, relaxed on his horse, but now his Colt is pointed at the kid in the pork pie hat. For an age all possibilities hang in the balance; then Ed repeats, "Ain't that right?"

"Yes. Yes. Sure. I won't cause any trouble."

The kid spits again and lowers his gun.

"You're crazy," he says under his breath.

"Maybe so," Ed replies, "but I still give the orders round here. Now, empty those saddlebags and let's see what he's got."

The kid pulls his hat down over his eyes and turns away. I suck in my first large breath in what feels like a lifetime.

"What 'bout 'is 'orse?" the one called Red asks.

"Leave it," Ed says. "Ain't worth much anyways."

In one fluid motion, Red raises his heavy rifle, cocks it and shoots Alita between the eyes. The explosion is deafening. Alita's head jerks up as if she is startled. She tries to move her feet and fails before she falls heavily on her side.

It happens so quickly I have no time to react other than to gasp, "Alita," in horror.

"What the hell d'you do that for?" Ed asks.

Red shrugs. "You didn't say to leave the horse alive, an' this way, the kid ain't gonna catch us up."

"You know that leaving a man in the desert without a horse is the same as killing him. How's he supposed to get back to the coast without a horse?"

Red shrugs again. "That'd be his problem."

I'm still staring stupidly at Alita's body when the Kid's heavy revolver catches me a solid blow to my left temple. Pain erupts behind my eyes and the world goes black.

W hen I come to, the sun is low in the western sky, and the blood on my arm and down the side of my face has caked to a stiff crust. Every movement sends bolts of pain through my head and explodes bright white lights behind my eyes. Slowly I manage to struggle into a sitting position.

Alita's body lies where it fell, her back to me and her head twisted back. Her eyes are open and seem to be staring at me. Her bridle, reins and saddle are gone. A black swarm of flies hover above her and are thick on the congealing pool of blood by her head. Two vultures are working at her stomach. Weakly I throw a rock at them, and they raise their bloody heads and waddle away a few feet.

Moving slowly and stopping frequently to ease the pain and allow my vision to clear, I stand up and look around. In addition to Alita's tack, my bedroll and saddlebags are gone. I still have my boots and clothes, but the pockets have been gone through and all my money stolen. I'm relieved to find the letter from my father still in my shirt. My blanket and hat lie on the ground nearby. At least they've left me something.

The sun has dropped behind the hills where I camped last night. It's still light, but there is a chill in the air. Gingerly I sit back down, put my hat on and lift my blanket. My empty canteen and the black tin revolver box lie beneath it. I open the box and take out my revolver, powder and bullets. Odd that they've left these things. I wonder if it was Ed who slipped them under the blanket. He was the only one who seemed reluctant to shoot me out of hand.

I move the chamber guard of the revolver aside and slowly begin loading it. It hurts to move my arm, but I need something to concentrate on. I pour a measured amount of powder into each chamber, followed by a wad of cotton and a bullet. I place a percussion cap in the opposite end of each chamber and close it. I load only five chambers, leaving the sixth beneath the hammer empty to avoid an accidental discharge. I tuck the revolver into my belt and close the box.

I'm not sure why I've done this, but the ritual calms me. As my confusion recedes, it is replaced by sorrow at losing Alita, my only friend in this land. Fighting back tears, I haul myself back to my feet and stagger over to a large rock about ten feet off the path. I wrap the blanket around my shoulders and sit with my back to the rock, feeling the day's warmth slowly seep into my shoulders.

I sit and wonder why I'm still alive. Of course, without a rifle, horse or any money, my chances of remaining alive long have taken a dramatic downturn. However, as the kid in the pork pie hat said, the easy and sensible thing for them to do, and the thing that he suggested they had done numerous times before, was to kill me. Why had Ed prevented him? It hardly seems likely that he has developed a fondness for me over the course of our few hours' traveling.

I shake my head and instantly regret it as my vision blurs and waves of nausea overwhelm me. When I recover, I begin to think about my more immediate concerns. What am I going to do?

For the moment, I have few choices. It's almost dark and the last thing I want to do in my present condition is stumble around blind in the desert. I'll wait here and hope I feel better in the morning. Then what?

I promised Ed I would head back to the coast, but how can I do that without a horse or supplies? Tucson isn't far, just over the pass in the next valley. It's the obvious place to go. I could report the robbery, assuming they have anything like police in this place, but what good would that do? How much effort is a sheriff going to put into searching for a gang who robbed a stupid kid from up north who has no good reason for even being here?

There's food in Tucson and replacements for all the things I've lost, but I have nothing to buy them with or trade for them. I still have my revolver. I could turn to robbery like Ed, but I probably wouldn't be very good at it, and anyway, why should some other poor traveler suffer just because I was unfortunate?

I could get a job, but what could I do? Work in a store and be stuck for the rest of my life behind a counter working for a few cents a day? I clench my fists in frustration and anger.

"Damn you, Ed," I shout into the gathering darkness. "You can't stop me. I'm *not* going back. I came down here with a purpose, and I'm not about to give up and run home with my tail between my legs at the first sign of trouble. I came down here to find my father and that's what I'm going to do."

I have no idea how I'm going to do this, but I feel better letting my anger out and with a decision made. I pull the blanket tighter against the growing cold.

It's a long night, and I do little more than doze for short periods only to awaken stiff and shivering. Several times I throw rocks at the squabbling vultures, but, as more arrive and coyotes show up to share in the pickings, they pay less and less attention to my weak efforts. Eventually, I leave them to it.

Sometimes I spend waking spells weeping for Alita, at other times I feel sorry for myself and regret ever leaving Yale. Although I wish I was back home, I hold on to my determination to go on. At other times I am almost overwhelmed by rage. I want revenge. I want Red to suffer for what he did to Alita, my friend who never hurt anyone. I want the Kid to feel the terror I felt with his gun cocked and pointed in my face. And I want Ed to know that I can't be fooled and betrayed so easily.

Oddly, as daylight arrives, I feel encouraged. My arm still hurts when I move it, but my head feels much better. I find a pool of ice-cold water in a rock hollow and carefully wash off the dried blood. I drink, fill my canteen and walk up the trail to the pass.

Below me, a wide valley is bathed in the morning sun. I stand for a minute and let the sun's rays warm me. On the far side of the valley a much larger range of mountains than the ones I have just crossed lie in shadow. They look daunting, but to my right I can see a trail or wagon road running toward what appears to be a wide pass.

Tucson's not large, a collection of dirt streets in the middle of the valley, but I can see square fields beside many of the houses and am ridiculously thrilled by this meager sign of civilization. Swamped by unjustifiable optimism, I set off downhill.

5

Judging by the height of the sun, it's near noon by the time I am walking along one of Tucson's dusty streets. It has been a slow progress dragging my pained body down from the hills. I am exhausted and hungry, but my headache has subsided to a dull throbbing.

The town is stretched north to south along the valley floor, so it is no more than four blocks wide in the direction I walk. Nevertheless, it has a prosperous appearance. I pass several well-maintained, white-washed adobe houses, a number of false-fronted stores and a respectable town hall.

Only a few people note my passing. Some children briefly stop playing with their clay marbles to watch me go by, and an old Mexican nods and murmurs, "*Buenos días.*" Across the street from the hotel there's a horse trough, and I go over to it, splash water on my face and fill my canteen. It's only when I straighten up that I notice the horses tethered to the rail in front of the hotel. One of them looks wild and, as I stare, turns its head to look at me. It has a white star on its forehead.

My heart skips a beat. I had assumed that Ed and the others would be miles away by now. The anger I felt in the night returns, but what am I going to do, face down a gang of killers in broad daylight? I examine the other horses. There's no sign of Ed's black gelding or the red-haired one's mount. Is the Kid alone?

Pulling my hat low over my face and tucking the revolver box under my left arm, I grip the handle of my gun and slowly cross the street. I ease up to the large window beside the front entrance and peer in. I'm looking into a long room with a bar down one side and scattered tables and chairs. One of the tables is occupied by four men playing cards. Three others stand along the bar. Two are strangers, the one in the middle is the kid in the pork pie hat. I pull back and lean against the wall of the hotel. What can I do?

I can barge into the hotel, waving my gun, and accuse the Kid of robbing me. In all likelihood, without Ed to restrain him, he will kill me and claim self-defense. I can look for the sheriff and have him arrested, but he will deny it and I have no proof. All that will do is alert the Kid and allow him to come after me as soon as the sheriff releases him. I could steal his horse and ride off, but that would be running away and would turn me into a horse thief, liable to be hanged if someone catches me.

An idea begins to take shape in my mind. I don't want to turn to a life of robbery to get what I need, but the Kid robbed me. He probably still has some of my money in his pocket, if he hasn't spent it all in the saloon. If I can head out of town, find a suitable spot and ambush him, then I can get back at least some of my things. Maybe enough money to keep going.

Pleased with my decision, I hurry down the street.

———◦———

I'm in a good spot, crouched among some large rocks as the trail turns and begins to climb into the hills east of Tucson. I can see almost all the way back to the town and will have plenty of warning of the Kid's approach, but I'm beginning to have doubts. What if he's planning on staying in Tucson for a couple of days? What if he's not alone? Ed and Red might have simply been somewhere else in town. What if he takes a different trail?

A part of me wouldn't mind it if he takes a different route out of town. I wouldn't have to face him and it wouldn't be my fault. I decide I'll give it until dark, and then I'll try and think of something else.

My stomach growls noisily. I sip some water and stare along the trail. Two men have passed since I sat here. Neither was the Kid and neither even noticed me. A third is coming along now, but he is no more than a shimmering dot in the lowering sun.

I remember what my mother said about knowing when to stay and fight and knowing when to run. Here I am, destitute, sitting in the middle of the desert waiting to ambush a brutal outlaw who would kill me as soon as spit. I should run, but I don't. Instead I tighten my grip on my revolver and stare along the trail.

Eventually the rider is close enough for me to make out his pork pie hat and the white star on his horse's head. I try to calm my breathing and remember my father saying that a revolver is only good at closer than a hundred feet. I want the Kid to get a lot closer than that, but the waiting is hell.

I'm relieved that the Kid is alone, but as he approaches, I realize a flaw in my ambush plan. The sun is setting behind him and in my eyes. He will be able to see me much better than I can see him. But there's not much I can do about that now.

I wait in an agony of anticipation until he is no more than twenty feet away, and then I stand up.

The horse shies at my sudden appearance, and the Kid has trouble controlling him. Eventually he calms his mount and stares hard at me.

"Wha'd'you wan'?" he slurs. With a shock, I realize that he's drunk. This gives me confidence.

"I want my money back," I demand as firmly as I can.

The Kid laughs. "Money back! Knew should've kilt you back there. Shtill time now." He sways sideways in his saddle and scrabbles with his right hand at the Colt in his belt.

"No," I say, raising my revolver and cocking the hammer. The cylinder rotates until a loaded chamber is aligned. "Don't do that. I don't want to shoot you."

I notice that the barrel of my gun is shaking back and forth. The Kid is only a dark silhouette against the evening sky.

"Shoot me? Can't shoot me." He has his Colt out now, but he's waving it around wildly.

"Stop," I say in desperation, but the Kid only laughs again. The long barrel waves toward me and there is a loud *click*. Either he has fired on an empty chamber or gone off at half cock.

"Damn," the Kid says and almost falls off backward. He drags on the reins and his horse dances around in a full circle. "Tha's be'er," he says, hauling back on the Colt's hammer.

I watch the cylinder rotate. The Kid is concentrating hard, and the gun is pointing straight at me, just like it was last night. Anger at the memory of my fear overwhelms me.

"No," I yell and pull the trigger.

We both fire at the same time, and the noise is deafening. The Kid's bullet explodes against the rock beside my head, and I feel needles of pain as fragments of lead and rock embed themselves in my cheek. The Kid's horse rears violently, throwing its rider to the ground. With a loud whinny, it bolts past me.

The Kid is lying on his back beside the trail, his eyes open. His hat has come off and rolled a short way down the hill, but he still clutches the Colt in his hand. There's a red stain on his shirt front. I kneel beside him and put my hand beneath his head to help him sit up. I feel wetness. It's only then that I notice the Kid's eyes aren't moving.

For a long time, as dusk turns to dark, I sit by the body. I've killed a man. I don't know if my bullet in his chest would have been fatal, but the rock that caved in the back of his skull certainly was, and both are my doing. I rationalize that it was self-defense, but then if I hadn't decided to lay up here and ambush him, none of this would have happened. I have ended a human life and revenge turns out to be not as sweet as I thought it would be.

Eventually, as the moon rises above the hills, I go through the Kid's pockets. There are only a few coins in them. I drag his body into a nearby hollow and pile as many rocks as I can find on top of him. It's not much of a grave, but I hope it will keep most animals off. I bury his Colt and his hat with him. Then I start walking.

6

I walk around in the hills most of the night, thinking about what I have done and how my life has changed so dramatically in just a few weeks. Back home I was the son of the lady who runs the stopping house in Yale. Here I'm nobody, a penniless vagabond killer whose life is worth nothing.

I used to feel in control. If I made a decision, things happened more or less as I expected. Here it's different; I'm like a leaf buffeted by the wind or swept along on a river current. When I decide something, I have no idea what the consequences will be. I feel almost helpless. If only I could go back and change things.

I try to follow trails in the dark, some of which must only be animal tracks, but I am hopelessly lost. After falling painfully several times and almost stumbling off the edge of a deep arroyo, I huddle behind a rock, wrap my blanket around me and try to sleep.

I guess I must have dozed because I wake up with the first rays of the sun on my face, cold, stiff and hungry. My arm, side and head still hurt from the original ambush, and an assortment of cuts and bruises have been added from my nocturnal adventures. In addition, my left cheek feels like it is on fire, and I feel dried blood crack when I move my jaw. I feel my cheek and wince as my palm rubs sharp pieces of rock. I pull a few out, but without a mirror it's too awkward and the pain soon makes me stop.

I drag myself to my feet, wrap my revolver box in my blanket and scramble down into an arroyo to look for water. I have no real aim, I simply want to feel better, emotionally and physically. I don't notice the old man until he speaks.

"*Buenos días, joven.*"

I try to grab my revolver box from my blanket, forgetting that the gun is in my belt, and I drop everything and fall painfully into a small barrel cactus.

I hear laughter, and embarrassment takes over from fear.

The old man is standing on the rim of the arroyo above me. He's wearing deerskin leggings, a colorful embroidered shirt and a faded blue army jacket. His hair is pure white and hangs long over his shoulders from beneath a strange helmet. The helmet has a high crown that runs fore and aft and a narrow brim that is peaked at the front and back. It's obviously very old and is rusted almost through in places. However, the rest of it is polished to a gleaming shine.

"What do you want?" I ask.

"*¿Qué quiero?*" he repeats my question and then switches effortlessly to English, which he speaks with a suggestion of an English accent. "I want nothing. It seems it is you who wants something." His face is the color of leather and there's not a square inch of it that's not as wrinkled and dry as this landscape. He has broad, high cheekbones and dark eyes that flash in the low sun.

"Are you an Apache?" I ask.

"Questions. Questions. Always questions with you white people. You cannot let the world be. You wish to know everything, even that which cannot be known. The answer is yes and no."

I look puzzled. The strange old man laughs. He lifts his right hand, turns the thumb toward himself and runs it down the length of his body.

"I am everything. This side"—he indicates his right side—"is Spanish, proud, strong. But my heart, *mi corazón*"—he pounds the left side of his chest—"is Apache. But I have lived with white men so long that my head is white." He slaps his forehead and laughs again. "And I too have learned how to ask a question. Would you like some tortillas and beans and coffee?"

"I would," I say, feeling myself smile despite everything. "Thank you."

"Do not thank me. I have given you nothing yet, *nada*. Now, young man, *joven*, get out of that cactus, pick up your things and follow me." The old man turns and strides off.

I grab my blanket and box and scramble out of the gully just in time to see the old man vanish around the hillside. Ignoring my aches, I hurry behind him.

After a considerable time struggling along a goat path that leads up the hillside—amazed at how fast the old man can move—I begin to wonder if I am being lured into a trap. But I've come too far to turn back now. Eventually we arrive at a spot where the path widens onto a ledge in front of the low entrance to a cave. The old man is already squatting by a pile of wood, striking a flint. He has taken his helmet off and placed it on the ground beside him.

"Go into the cave and meet my *compadre*, Perdido," he says. "He gave me my helmet, *mi casco*."

I put down my blanket but hesitate. What if it's a trap? I place my hand on the handle of my revolver.

The old man chuckles.

"You will not need your *pistola*. Perdido is harmless, I assure you."

Flames are already licking at the smaller branches by the time I pluck up the courage to bend down at the cave entrance. The entrance is small, but inside the cave opens out to the size of a small room. It takes a moment for my eyes to adjust to the gloom. The first thing I see is the old man's bed, a long pile of brushwood with a blanket on top. There's an unstrung bow, a quiver of arrows, an ax and a collection of various-sized clay pots around it.

I look to my left where I can just make out a lance and an ancient musket leaning against the wall. Unexpectedly, there is also a thick book, which I assume to be a bible until my eyes adjust enough to read the title,

Moby Dick. It's not a volume I have read, but I know the name very well. My father used to tell me a story of a white whale of that name and the obsession of a man called Ahab who searched the oceans for it. It's strangely unsettling to see the whale's name on a book here in this primitive setting.

Preoccupied, I let my gaze wander back around the cave. From my right, a grinning skull stares back at me.

I almost scream in fear but control it to a loud gasp. I hear the old man outside chuckle. The skeleton is sitting on the floor, leaning against the cave wall. One arm has fallen off and lies beside it, but the rest is held together by dark brown stringy tendons. Perdido is wearing sandals woven from grass, the remnants of a pair of leather pants and a rusted, short-sleeved chain-mail shirt. There's a narrow sword lying on his lap and a plain cross hanging from a chain around his neck. Perdido has obviously been a soldier, but for whom and from when, I have no idea. I make my way back out into the sunshine.

"Who is he?" I ask the old man, who is now squatting by the fire, placing a flat iron sheet between two rocks over the flames.

"He is Perdido. I told you."

"But where is he from? What happened to him? What is his story?" I move over and crouch beside the fire.

"Ah. So now you want stories, *historias*. That is the difficulty with you white people: you always want more." He reaches over and places a battered tin pot filled with beans on a flat rock in the fire.

"Do you know how valuable stories are?"

"Yes," I say, not certain that I do.

"Huh," the old man snorts dismissively. "I do not think so. The world exists in two places. Here, *aquí*." He sweeps a scrawny arm wide to encompass the world. "Now, *ahora*, this moment of pain, and hunger, and sunshine, and darkness, and death, *muerte*. And here." He touches a finger to his temple. "Where yesterday lives."

I frown in puzzlement, and the old man leans forward and deftly flips a tortilla on his makeshift griddle.

"You are like children, *niños*, you white men. You need everything explained. Your meeting in my cave with Perdido, it exists no more. It was only real when you were face to face. It is gone now and cannot be recaptured. It lives only in your head. It has become a story. Part of your story, and of Perdido's.

"You are now the guardian of that story. You may tell it. You may change it. It does not matter; it is your story now. But with stories comes responsibility. The past, *el pasado*, exists only in our stories. Change the story and you change the past. Stories are the only way the past can live; that is their power. Do not ask for or tell them lightly.

"Can you read words?" he asks abruptly.

"Yes," I reply.

"And write words?"

I nod.

"That is good. Stories become more real if they are written on paper. I have a story written on paper."

"*Moby Dick*," I say. "I saw it in your cave."

"I am told it is of a sea monster and the man who searches for it."

"It is."

"And that it begins with a name."

"It does. Ishmael."

"That is good," the old man says thoughtfully. "Names are important. But it is time to eat," he says, lifting two large, flat pieces of thick bark from beside the fire. "Good stories are best told on a full belly."

The old man concentrates on spooning beans onto the pieces of bark. He adds tortillas to each and passes one over to me. I watch and try to copy as he deftly wraps the tortilla round the beans and eats. My eating is much messier, but the food tastes good.

We eat in silence until the pot of beans is empty and wiped clean with the last of the tortillas. Then the old man pours a black liquid into a tin mug. It is the only mug he has and so we share. The coffee is bitter, but I feel restored by the hot drink.

"Now we must know each other," the old man says, sitting back. He pulls a tobacco pouch from his belt, undoes the neck and pours some dark leaves onto a torn piece of an old newspaper. He rolls it, twists the two ends and places one end in his mouth. Reaching forward, he plucks a burning stick from the fire, tilts his head to one side and lights the other end of his cigarette. He puffs and looks at me.

"What is your name?"

"My name is James Doolen," I reply.

"Hmmm. This name, James Doolen." The old man says my name slowly, savoring the sounds. "What does it mean?"

"I don't know," I say. "I've never thought about it. I don't think it means anything."

"Then it is not a name," he scoffs and takes a long drag on his cigarette. "A name must have meaning or it is nothing. If you do not have a name, then you have no center, and if you have no center, then how can you know where you are or where you are going?

"I gave Perdido his name when he became my friend. It was my gift to him in exchange for his helmet. Do you know what it means?"

Suddenly I realize I do know what it means. "Lost."

The old man smiles.

"Exactly. Perdido is lost, to his family, his compadres, his world. Now, I will give you a real name." He tilts his head and stares at me until I begin to feel uncomfortable. Eventually he says, "From now on you shall be Busca."

"Busca," I try out the sound. "What does it mean?"

"I think that you are searching for something," the old man says. "In Perdido's language, *uno quien busca* is one who seeks; therefore, you shall be Busca."

"Thank you," I say, strangely pleased with my new name. "What is your name?"

"If you live as many years as I, you collect many names. My mother was Chiricahua Apache, an aunt of Firewood, the warrior you know as Cochise, and she gave me my first name, Too-ah-yay-say."

"Tooaysay," I say, struggling with the complex pronunciation.

My companion smiles.

"It is, I think, difficult for your ears. It means Strong Swimmer. I earned it as a boy, in the first year of your century, for the time I swam the Rio Grande River to recover a horse that had run away. Too-ah-yay-say."

"Too-ah-yay-say," I try again after the old man has repeated his name slowly. My pronunciation is awkward and halting, but I do better.

"Good, but Too-ah-yay-say is only my first name. My father was Spanish. This land was all New Spain when I was born, but he gave me no name. You see, I began life living in two worlds.

"And I have been called many things over the years, some good, some not so good, but I have one name in your tongue. It was given to me by an Englishman for whom I was a hunting guide many years ago and who taught me to speak your language. He called me Wellington." The old man placed the emphasis heavily on the final syllable. "I think it is after a famous warrior of his people. Perhaps you know him?"

"I have heard of him," I say, forcing myself not to smile. "He was a great general."

Wellington nods approval.

"That is the name I use today and by which you may call me. But now it is time for stories. Perdido's story

54

is lost, but I can tell you my story and Perdido's where it is a part of mine. Will you respect Perdido and my story?"

"Yes," I answer.

"And will you tell me your story in exchange?"

"Yes," I repeat.

"Very well then, Busca. Let us exchange stories. My story begins with this." He thumps his chest over his heart. "My Apache half."

"This land is very ancient," Wellington begins his tale. "*Antiguo*, and many people have passed through it. The old ones carved pictures on the rocks and built houses of mud that dwarf the puny things you white men build of wood, many lifetimes before even my mother's people arrived here. Their stories are vanished." He looks sad at the thought of all the lost stories.

"When I was a child, my grandfather told me of something that happened when his grandfather's grandfather's grandfather was but a *niño*." Wellington waves his arms as if to emphasize how long ago that must have been.

"In those far-off days some men came to our land from the south. They were white men and they rode the first horses my people had ever seen. Some said they were gods because they carried spears that flashed fire and some wore suits made of metal that glinted in the sun, but they were not gods, they were just different men. They were led by a man called Coronado, and they had wonders that we did not know of—horses, guns and armor—but all their wonders were things, and without them they had little.

"We had few things—a sharp arrow point, a good club—but we had something more valuable: knowledge. They did not know where to find water or how to catch and skin a lizard for dinner. They did not know how to live in the desert, and without that what good are all the wonders of the world?" Wellington stares at me as if he expects an answer, but when I stay silent, he continues.

"They came to our villages and asked about a city of gold, *una ciudad del oro*. We said we did not know, but perhaps there were such things to the north where we had not been. I do not know if they believed us, but they left.

"Some of our young men followed them, and when they saw how these newcomers did not know how to live in the desert, they wanted to kill them and steal their wonders. The elders said that only bad would come of molesting these men and it would be best to let them pass through, but young men do not always listen to advice.

"Some warriors followed the strangers and ambushed small parties that left the main group to hunt or search for their city of gold. They brought horses and weapons back to our villages. The elders were not happy, but the strangers did not return to claim their things. The young men said that all the stranger's power was in their things, and without them they were weak. In any case, we never saw them again; but, although my ancestors never knew it, our world had changed.

"We learned to ride the horses and breed them, and this helped us greatly with our hunting and fighting our enemies, but other strangers came from the south and brought cattle and sheep with them and took over our land and put up fences and built houses and towns and churches. We fought them for many years, but there were too many. We tried to take away their possessions to make them powerless, but it did not work. It seemed that however many horses we ran off or guns we stole, there were always more.

"For all that, we learned to live with these strangers. We raided and killed some of them, and they raided and killed some of us, but the land was big enough for all. And they are my other half." Wellington sweeps his hand down the right side of his body. "It was on one of these raids that a Mexican, as these new Spaniards called themselves, found my mother hiding in an arroyo and became my father."

Wellington pauses and takes a deep breath as if preparing himself for the next part of his story.

"Then more strangers came from the north," he continued eventually. "*Americanos.* They fought with both the men from the south and with us, and much blood soaked into the desert.

"The Americanos are a part of my story. I have fought against them, as some of my people still do, but we will not defeat the north men. They are like ants on the desert floor. You can kill many by standing on them, but more will always come."

Wellington stops talking and I assume he is finished. The men from the south must have been Coronado's Spanish conquistadores followed by the Mexicans and the Americans. I am wondering if it's my turn to tell a story when the old man continues.

"I did my share of fighting when I was young. I knew the great warriors—my cousin, Cochise, and Red Sleeves, Mangas Coloradas—but I saw how many soldiers there were and how they kept coming, no matter how many we killed."

A look of great sadness crosses Wellington's face.

"It was not a good time. I saw forests of poles hung with our drying scalps and how the white men paid each other money for them. It is one thing to take a trophy when you kill a brave warrior in a good fight, but these white men killed women and children for their hair. When I saw all this, I knew we could not win against these people. So I left my people and went to work for the white men.

"I was a guide for an Englishman with many names who came to our land to hunt," Wellington pauses and concentrates. "Lord Alfred George Cambrey Sommerville, Earl of Canterbury," he says in one breath. "I do not think his names meant anything, but he set much store by them. He taught me his language and killed many lions before my people found him.

"Lord Alfred George Cambrey Sommerville, Earl of Canterbury, went one day to follow a lion that was only wounded. He told me to stay at our camp, but I followed at a distance and watched. He was crouched by a rock, waiting for the lion to appear. I saw a small band of my people come close to him without him knowing.

"The first arrow hit Lord Alfred George Cambrey Sommerville, Earl of Canterbury, in the back. He roared in anger, stood up and turned. He fired his rifle and wounded one of the attackers. He did not have a chance to reload, although it took seven more arrows before he fell and my people could come close and end it with their knives and clubs."

Wellington pauses thoughtfully.

"He was a great warrior, even though he did not have a proper name.

"After that, I became a scout for the blue army in the great war that was fought between the states. I scouted the enemy ambush at Picacho Pass, but the young Lieutenant Barrett didn't listen and went forward anyway. The price was his life and that of several of his men."

Wellington shrugs as if the stupidity of the world is not his concern.

"Eventually I came to see that men are all the same. It makes little difference whether they are white or red, or black like the buffalo soldiers I saw once. Some are good, some are bad, but all die alone.

So I decided to give up the company of men and live alone in the desert.

"One day, I found this cave, crawled in and saw Perdido. I think he was one of the long-ago southerners, maybe even one who accompanied Coronado on his search for golden cities. Perhaps he was wounded by our young warriors and managed to drag himself here before he died.

"I liked Perdido immediately. He understood loneliness. I made my home in his cave and we became friends. Occasionally others, such as yourself, come to visit, but Perdido and I are content."

The old man again lapses into silence and sips his coffee.

"That's quite a story," I say. Remembering something Ed told me, I ask, "Did you know of a scalp hunter called Roberto Ramirez?"

The old man looks at me sharply.

"Always more questions," he says. "Was my story so much not to your liking that you wish more?"

"Yes. No," I say in confusion. "It was a good story. I liked it very much. It was very interesting."

Wellington seems mollified.

"Then you owe me a story, as you promised."

"Of course." I launch into the tale of my journey down here. I skim over the early parts, but when I tell him of the schooner, the *Robert Boswell*, on which I sailed to San Diego, he nods vigorously and says, "Yes. Yes. I have heard of such vessels."

I concentrate on the meeting with Ed, the ambush and my killing the kid in the pork pie hat. Wellington listens closely and occasionally nods as if confirming that I have got the details right.

When I finish, he nods approval.

"That was a good story, thank you. I shall remember it. That way, even if you die tomorrow, you will live on in what time I have left to remember."

Wellington stands and stretches stiffly.

"But now we must tend to your wounds." Without waiting for an answer, he heads off down the mountainside. I scramble to my feet and follow.

At length, we come to a spring coming out of a cleft in the rock. It's not a rushing torrent and it quickly soaks into the sands of the arroyo below, but enough water flows to fill a small hollow in the rock. Wellington makes me kneel beside the pool and gently washes the blood off my face. Then he carefully picks out the pieces of rock and bullet embedded in my cheek. It's a painful process, but when it's done, I feel better.

When he is satisfied that he has cleaned everything, Wellington takes a few small dried leaves out of a pouch on his belt, puts them in his mouth and chews vigorously. When he is satisfied, he takes the soggy mess out and plasters it over my wounds. It feels soothing.

"Now you must sleep," he says, shepherding me back up the mountain and onto his sleeping pallet in the cave. I don't even have time to think about sharing the cave with Perdido before I am asleep.

The sun is still high in the sky when I wake up and crawl out of the cave, so it can't be much past noon.

I can't have slept more than a couple of hours, but the effect of the rest and the food is amazing. My injuries still ache, but I feel revitalized and eager to go on. Wellington is crouching by the fire and greets me as I stand and stretch.

"You do not sleep long, Busca. That is good. Sleep is the little death, *la pequeña muerte*, and the end comes soon enough without it." He stands up. "Come, I have your horse."

Wellington strides off without giving me a chance to ask what he means. I don't have a horse, Alita's dead.

Confused, I hurry after Wellington, down into a narrow arroyo where a few gnarled mesquite trees have pushed their roots sufficiently deep into the desert ground to find enough water to support life. Where the arroyo widens at its mouth stands a horse, its head low and its reins dragging on the ground. It has white star on its forehead.

"That's not my horse," I say. "It belonged to the man I shot."

I feel guilt returning at the memory.

"And, any minute now, he will be walking up the arroyo to claim it back?" Wellington asks. "You took his life, so his horse is yours. And who else will take it? I have no use for a horse in these mountains. Would you rather it wander until a mountain lion finds it?"

"Of course not," I say.

Wellington shrugs. "Then take it. If you happen to run into the kid again, you can give the horse back to him."

I can't argue. The alternative is to let the horse run wild, and I do need a horse. I take a couple of steps forward. The horse raises its head, stamps its hooves and eyes me warily.

"It's okay, boy," I say in a quiet voice as I hold out my hand and slowly move closer. "I'm not going to hurt you. We can become friends. I have a long journey ahead and you can help."

The horse rolls its eyes back until the white is showing, throws its head up and whinnies through bared teeth. It takes a couple of skittering steps backward and stands looking at me with wide eyes. I repeat the process, but the result is the same.

"Busca," Wellington says behind me. "You must explain things to him."

"What do you mean?" I ask.

Wellington sighs, as if he is dealing with a not-very-intelligent child, and steps past me. He approaches the horse slowly, speaking in the strange, complex language of his original name. In fact, I hear his name, Too-ah-yay-say, mentioned several times. The horse watches him closely and shifts its feet but doesn't retreat. Wellington strokes the animal's forehead and puts his head beside its ear, talking all the time. A shudder ripples down the horse's flanks but it doesn't move.

For an age, Wellington strokes and talks to the horse. Occasionally he looks over at me and I hear my name, but mostly I have no idea what Wellington is saying.

Eventually he looks up and says, "Come over here, Busca."

Slowly I step forward. The horse watches me suspiciously but stays where it is. It even lets me stroke its head.

"What did you say?" I ask.

"I told him your story. I told him that his previous owner was partly responsible for your horse's death and that you had killed his owner. These are things he knew already, but I explained that they meant that he is now yours. He agreed that this is the case, and he hopes that you will treat him better than his previous owner."

"I will," I say, trying hard not to think about how Wellington knows what the horse is thinking.

"Then you must tell him so. And also explain where you will go and what you will ask him to do."

"I have come down here to look for my father," I say, feeling awkward talking to the horse as if he was another person, "and I would like your help with that."

The horse nuzzles my cheek as if he understands and agrees.

"I was angry after your old owner and the others killed my horse," I continue. "Her name was Alita. That is why I lay in wait for your owner and killed him, but now my anger is gone. We won't go and search for the others, but go down to Casas Grandes, which is the only clue I have about my father."

The more I talk the more comfortable I feel. The horse continues to nuzzle my cheek.

"That is good," Wellington says when I finish. "Horses need good stories as much as people do. They have their own stories and many are about the men who brought them to this land in their search for cities of gold. Perhaps, if you listen well, this horse will tell you his story.

"Now there is one other thing you must do. Give your new friend a name."

I think for a minute. "I will call him Coronado after the man who led the army that brought the horses to this land."

The horse pushes against me and Wellington nods. "Coronado," he says. "It is a good strong name. Now you must go."

I feel upset that Wellington is dismissing me so abruptly. I have enjoyed my short time here, but I know I must move on. And now that I have a horse, there is no point in delaying. I tether Coronado to a branch and follow Wellington back up to his cave to collect my pistol and blanket. I crawl in to say goodbye to Perdido. When I come out Wellington hands me the battered copy of *Moby Dick*.

"You must take this story," he says. "Lord Alfred George Cambrey Sommerville, Earl of Canterbury, gave it to me, but I cannot read the words. He began to teach me but he died before I could learn much. I am too old now for such tricks, so you should have Ishmael's story of the sea monster."

"Thank you," I say, touched by the gesture. "I shall treasure it."

Wellington nods and we return to Coronado.

The Kid's saddle is old and worn but serviceable. I take down his bedroll and saddlebags. I don't intend to sleep in a dead man's bedroll, but it is heavy so I unroll it. Inside is a double-barreled scatter gun like the ones I have seen the guards on stagecoaches carrying. This one has both the stock and the barrel cut down severely so that the weapon is not much more than two feet long. It wouldn't be much good at any distance, but at close range, filled with buckshot, it would be devastating.

I go through the pockets of the saddlebags. There's not much in them—a flint, some tobacco, some dried beans, a bag with a mix of a few silver dollars and some pesos, some bullets for the Kid's Colt revolver and a few scatter-gun shells, and a half-empty whiskey bottle. I give Wellington the Colt ammunition, the beans and the tobacco, and smash the whiskey bottle against a rock.

I'm about to pack my meager belongings, when I notice something else. At the bottom of one pocket lies a silver locket. It's oval, almost the length of my thumb and covered in intricate engraving. There is a silver chain looped through a ring at one end.

I undo the clasp and am suddenly staring at the faces of two fair-haired women. They are both dressed formally and are obviously related, although one is about my age and the other significantly older. I guess mother and daughter. Despite the formality of having their pictures taken, both are smiling gently at the camera.

The thought of this happy pair being the Kid's mother and sister shocks me. I barely imagined him as human, let alone having a family that would miss and mourn him. I guiltily snap the locket closed and stuff it back in the saddlebag.

"You go to Casas Grandes?" Wellington asks when I have finished packing and am ready to mount.

"It's the only clue to where my father might be," I say.

Wellington nods. "That is good. Follow the arroyo out into the valley. Keep the rising sun over your left shoulder for five days until you reach the village of Esqueda. There you must turn to face the rising sun for five more days as you cross the mountains. Then you will be at Casas Grandes."

"Thank you, Wellington," I say, feeling sad at leaving the old man. "For everything."

Wellington shrugs. "*No es nada*. What are a few tortillas and beans. I thank you for your story."

There seems nothing more to say, yet I have trouble leaving. Eventually Wellington speaks again.

"You asked if I knew the scalp hunter named Roberto Ramirez."

"I did," I say.

"I knew of him," Wellington says.

"Was he as evil as some say?" I ask.

Wellington shrugs.

"People say many things, but one must think of who is doing the saying. Is the word of an evil person to be taken the same as that of one who is good?

"Be careful of names. Some men do not understand their importance. They think a name is like a gun: it can be stolen and used for good or evil by whoever possesses it. They are wrong. You may steal a name, but you can never own it. I am not so clever that I can judge this Roberto Ramirez, whoever he may be."

Wellington pauses and I am about to ask for more detail when he says, "You must go. Perdido and I wish you well on your journey, Busca, and hope your search is fruitful."

Wellington turns on his heel and strides back up the gully toward his cave and his long-dead companion. Reluctantly I turn Coronado's head and we walk down the arroyo and out onto the next wide, dry valley.

I sit on Coronado, watching the column of dust move slowly toward me over the wide, empty valley bottom. I don't think it's a threat, and there's nowhere to hide out here even if it is. It's the second day since I said farewell to Wellington, and I am traveling more or less southeast down a dry valley with rugged hills in the distance on both sides. I can't be far from the Mexican border. Eventually the shapes at the base of the dust resolve themselves into a column of soldiers. I encourage Coronado and we trot forward to meet them.

"Good day," the young officer at the head of the column greets me as he raises his hand to bring his men to a halt. He is white, but the twenty or so men behind him are black, although it's hard to tell them apart through the thick layer of dust covering them and their mounts.

"I'm Lieutenant Fowler of B Company, Tenth US Cavalry, on patrol chasing savages out of Fort Bowie. Who might you be and where you headed?"

"My name's James Doolen, and I'm headed down to Mexico."

Lieutenant Fowler stares hard at me for a long moment.

"Can't imagine why you'd want to go down there," he says eventually, "but I reckon that'd be your business. What I will do is give you a bit of advice.

"Sergeant Rawlins," the Lieutenant shouts back over his shoulder. "Show this young man what we're carrying on them mules."

After some commotion farther down the column, a large man with sergeant's stripes just visible through the dirt on his sleeves rides up leading two mules, each of which has a long military-cape-covered bundle draped over it. The sergeant nods at me and lifts the corner of the cape on the nearest mule.

The man's shirt and neck are covered in dried blood. There are a few strands of straggling brown hair still attached to the scalp, but the top of the head is a raw mass of bloody flesh.

I tense at the sight, which causes Coronado to skitter a few steps to the side. The sergeant moves to the second bundle and repeats the procedure. I know what's coming this time so I am somewhat prepared, but I still gasp in shock.

The second body is just as bloody as the first, but it has a wide band of blood-stiffened hair still attached above the right ear. The hair is a striking red.

"The red-haired man," I say before I have a chance to think.

"You know this fellow?" the Lieutenant asks.

"I don't know," I reply. "Maybe. I was robbed a few days back by someone with hair that color."

"Could be him right enough. I ain't never seen hair that color on any other soul round here, living or dead. Perhaps the savages did us a favor this time."

I look back at the other body, but the cape has fallen back. Is that Ed? The hair was right, what there was of it, but I don't want to get down and examine the body any closer.

"What happened to them?" I ask.

"Damned Apaches got them," the lieutenant says. "In the hills down by the border. We found them by an old campfire with more holes in them than a pincushion.

"First I reckoned they were prospectors. Plenty of hopefuls down that way following the stories of gold and silver in the hills." The officer sweeps his arm to the south and spits in the dust. "If you ask me, the only worthwhile rock they'll find'll be a tombstone.

"Anyways, these fellows had no rock samples, claim stakes or prospecting kit with them, so now I ain't so sure. Could be as you say, that they were road agents on the run or just trying to hide out. Whoever they were, we'll take them up to Bowie and get them buried afore they get to smelling too bad."

"Did you see the Apaches?" I ask. "Are they still in the hills?"

"No sign of them." The officer shakes his head. "But that don't mean nothing. You can ride ten feet away from a savage and never know he's there. Could be that they've moved on though. I reckon they were some young bucks broke out of the San Carlos reservation after Victorio flew the coop. Probably heading down to Mexico, looking to meet up with him or Geronimo. That's just fine by me. If they murder a few folk down that way, then it's the Federales' problem, not mine."

I feel uncomfortable with the lieutenant's dismissal of the Apaches as savages. Wellington was one of the most civilized people I have ever met, and the red-haired corpse, if he was the man who shot poor old Alita, and the Kid were immeasurably more savage than him.

"Sergeant"—the lieutenant turns to the black man beside him—"take them mules back to the rear of the column and get the men ready to move on."

"Yes, sir." The sergeant hauls the mules around and heads back down the line of soldiers.

"You're more than welcome to accompany us to Bowie," the lieutenant says.

"Thank you," I reply, "but I think I'll keep heading on."

"Suit yourself," he says, "but travel fast and keep your eyes open. Nights'd be the best time to move. Where you headed in Mexico?"

"Casas Grandes. I was told to head south for Esqueda and then turn east."

"That'll work. The end of this valley, couple of hours' ride, that's the border. The valley splits round some hills, take the left fork. You'll come to a river. Follow it until you come out into a wide north-south valley and head south. That'll take you to Esqueda. Rest up good there because it's rough country from

Esqueda over to Casas Grandes. Good luck and keep a weather eye out for the savages."

"Thank you."

Lieutenant Fowler nods, wheels his horse and resumes his position at the head of the column. He raises his hand and orders, "Move out."

Amidst the clanking of bits and the slow drumming of hooves, the column moves past me. Several of the soldiers turn to look at me, and Sergeant Rawlins nods as he passes.

As the dust settles around me, I wonder why I didn't take the lieutenant up on his offer of an escort north to Fort Bowie. It would have been the safe and sensible thing to do. I suppose that my search for my father is such a strange and uncertain thing, and is turning out to be so much harder and more complex than I had imagined, that my resolve is hanging by a thread. I have to force myself to keep going. If I turn back to the relative comforts of Fort Bowie, I may never pluck up the courage to set out again. The goal of finding my father, or at least discovering what happened to him, has to drive me forward relentlessly or I will fail and spend the rest of my life wondering.

On top of that, I didn't like the way the lieutenant talked about the Apaches. Of course, I might think differently if I run into a band of them determined to take my scalp. I sigh and encourage Coronado into a trot away from the soldiers.

I take the left-forking valley as the sun lowers toward the horizon behind my right shoulder. I suppose I am in Mexico now, although I have seen nothing to suggest it. By the time dusk falls, I am crossing rougher ground and have reached the headwaters of a small river flowing in the direction I am traveling.

I move slowly in the dark, even after an almost-full moon rises to cast a ghostly silver light over everything. I imagine every shadow conceals a warrior ready to fire an arrow into my chest or leap up and cave in my skull with an ax. My scalp itches as I try not to imagine a knife blade scraping round my skull.

I'm cold and scared riding through the dark, but I'm more frightened of stopping and going to sleep. The trail by the river is narrow, and in places I can almost reach out and touch the trees beside it, but it is fairly flat and the valley bottom often widens out so that I feel a little less hemmed in. I wrap my blanket around my shoulders, and Coronado and I trudge on.

My head jerks upright and I almost fall out of the saddle. I've been asleep. Not for long, but the last thing I want to do is fall and injure myself. I rein in Coronado, uncork my canteen and splash water on my face. The shock of the water helps, but a few minutes after we start moving again, I find myself nodding off.

"Stay awake," I tell myself out loud. "You'd feel a fool if you travel at night to avoid an Apache attack, only to break your arm falling off your horse."

Talking out loud feels good.

"Well, Coronado, I hope Wellington…" I stop and think. "Too-ah-yay-say," I say. Somehow it seems right to use his Apache name after what Lieutenant Fowler said about savages. "I hope Too-ah-yay-say was right and that one day you'll tell me your story. I would like to hear more about your namesake and his explorations. Come to think of it, you could probably tell me a lot about the Apaches as well."

I think back over all the old man told me.

"You know, Coronado, Too-ah-yay-say is Cochise's cousin and he knew Mangas Coloradas. I read dime novels about them. Cochise was a great warrior and so was Mangas Coloradas. One story I read said that Mangas Coloradas went to talk peace under a flag of truce and was captured by the soldiers. While he was sleeping that night, the soldiers stabbed him with red-hot bayonets. When the warrior jumped up, they shot him and said he was trying to escape.

"What do you think of that, Coronado? And it's even worse. After they killed him, they boiled the flesh off his head and sent his skull back to a museum in Washington. That's more savage than scalping.

"I can hardly believe that Too-ah-yay-say knew these famous people and did all the things he said, fought in the war and led that Englishman on hunting trips. Too-ah-yay-say must be..."

I don't notice the tall figure until it steps out into the full moonlight and speaks. "What do you know of Too-ah-yay-say, K'uu-ch'ish and Dasoda-hae, whom you call Mangas Coloradas?"

Coronado skitters sideways and I almost fall off. The idea of turning and galloping off into the darkness crosses my mind, but it's insanity. There's no way I can stay on Coronado moving at high speed in the dark, even if he doesn't break a leg, and besides, other figures are detaching themselves from the shadows all around.

"I met Too-ah-yay-say in the mountains. He gave me tortillas and beans and cleaned my wounds and gave me directions to here. I'm on my way to

Casas Grandes." I'm speaking very fast, almost babbling as my fear mounts.

The man in front of me is a frightening sight. He's big, at least six feet tall and broad across the shoulders. His trousers disappear into soft leather boots that reach almost to his knees, and he wears a long loose shirt, belted at the waist with a broad red sash in which is tucked a long knife. His black hair hangs over his shoulders and is held off his face by another red sash wrapped around his head. He wears a full cartridge belt slung diagonally across his chest and a rifle over his left shoulder. In is right hand he holds a long lance from which hang an assortment of feathers and, I am appalled to see, a fresh red-haired scalp. He's smiling, but it could be at the pleasure of adding my scalp to his collection.

"Too-ah-yay-say told me he was a cousin of K'uu-ch'ish." I try to pronounce the name the way the warrior had. "He told me stories of Mangas Coloradas, Dosada-hay."

"Dasoda-hae," the stranger corrects me. "Too-ah-yay-say told you his story?"

"Yes, he did," I say hurriedly.

"Hmmmm. And you told him your story?"

"I did. I told him how I had come down here from the north to look for my father and how—"

"Do not be so eager to tell strangers your story. What other story did Too-ah-yay-say tell you?"

I struggle to work out what this man means. Too-ah-yay-say only told me one story, his. Then I realize. "He told me Perdido's story."

"And you met Perdido?"

"I did."

The man falls silent, and I can't think of anything to say. I shiver and it's not with cold. Any moment now I expect the pain of arrows or bullets piercing my back and feel the knife in the stranger's belt slicing my scalp off. To my utter surprise, the man bursts out laughing.

"So, the old fool still keeps that dried-up corpse in his cave, does he?" he asks as soon as he has calmed a bit.

"Yes," is all I can think to say.

The warrior walks forward until he stands beside me. The fresh red-haired scalp is hanging at face level not two feet from my eyes. "I took this two days past," he says, waggling the scalp. "It is a good color, is it not?"

"Yes, it is," I agree quickly.

"Tonight, I intended to take your hair to adorn my lance beside it. I followed you and listened to you talk to your horse. At first I thought you were a crazy man, and I was not happy. It is bad luck to take the hair of a crazy man, but then I heard you talk of Too-ah-yay-say and knew you were not crazy. But I cannot take the hair of one who has shared stories with Too-ah-yay-say."

"You know him?"

"All know Too-ah-yay-say. He is the keeper of stories. What is your name?"

"My old name was James Doolen, but Too-ah-yay-say gave me a new one: Busca."

"Busca." The warrior savors the sound. "A seeker, that is a good name and names are important. My name is Nah-kee-tats-an. It means two deaths. My father gave it to me after I fell in the river and drowned. When I was pulled out, all thought me dead, but my father held me upside down and thumped the water out of me and allowed the air back in. He said I was lucky. Because I had died once, it would be a long time before the Gods wished to see me again, so I would have a long life.

"You are lucky as well, Busca, that your hair does not now hang from my lance. I wish you well in your search."

Nah-kee-tats-an holds up his hand. I take it and his grip almost crushes my bones. I squeeze back as hard as I can.

"Don't go north," I say, remembering the lieutenant and his talk of savages. "There are soldiers there."

"I do not fear soldiers, but thank you." He releases my hand. "Goodbye, Busca." He takes a step but then turns back to look at me. "And yes," he says. "The story you read of Dasoda-hae's death was a true one."

In three strides, he has disappeared into the shadows. I turn round, but every other figure has vanished as well. Shaking with relief, but also strangely honored by the encounter, I dismount and lead Coronado down to the water's edge. There we drink before I unsaddle him, hobble him beside some lush grass and curl up in my blanket at the base of a willow. I am asleep in moments.

I wake up shivering to see tendrils of mist drifting over the river and twisting through the trees. I debate lighting a fire to warm up, but Coronado is standing beside me snorting, telling me it's time to get moving. It's two days since I met Nah-kee-tats-an and almost time to leave the river and head south for Esqueda. I eat the last couple of handfuls of beans that I cooked two days before, drink from the river and fill my canteen. Then Coronado and I go through our morning ritual.

Normally I would brush down my horse before saddling him, but I don't have a brush, so I stroke Coronado with my hand, removing any burrs, knots of hair or twigs he has picked up in the night. As I do this, I talk to him, telling him about any dreams I had the night before. This morning I don't remember any dreams.

"We were lucky the other night," I say. "At least I was. I reckon if I'd been scalped you would've become an Apache pony. Would you have liked that?"

Coronado turns his head and nuzzles me.

"Well, that's nice. There I'd be dead on the ground, my hair hanging from Nah-kee-tats-an's lance and off you go quite happily to your new life without a backward glance. Don't expect me to buy you a sack of grain in Esqueda for the ride over the mountains. Although, I don't suppose I should blame you. Your life with the Apaches would probably be quite good."

I pause for a moment and reflect on the past few days.

"Odd, the Apaches we've met are nothing like the ones I read about in the dime novels, or the way that Lieutenant Fowler saw them. I suppose there's good and bad, and maybe we just got lucky with the ones we met, but they don't seem like the savage killers everyone says they are. If the stories about the scalp hunters and Dasoda-hae are true, they've a right to be angry."

I place the saddle blanket on Coronado's back and then the saddle. I reach beneath him and grab the cinch straps. "Now, are we going to play this game again?" Coronado stamps his foot in answer.

I discovered the first time I saddled Coronado that he has a sense of humor. As soon as he feels the saddle on his back, he takes in a deep breath and swells his belly and chest. If I don't wait for him to breathe out before I tighten the cinch, it will be loose and I will end up in an unceremonious heap when I try to mount. It's amazing how long Coronado can hold his breath.

"Okay," I say, holding the cinch ready to tighten it, "I can wait."

Coronado turns his head and looks at me. He snorts out a breath that clouds the cold air.

"You're not going to catch me that way. That wasn't a full breath."

I stand and wait, and wait, and wait. Coronado becomes restless, shuffling from one forefoot to the other. At last he exhales a huge cloud of steam. I yank the cinch tight before he can breathe in again.

"Got you," I say triumphantly. "I know your tricks. I'll always outlast you in a waiting game."

Coronado shakes his head and snorts. I finish packing up, mount up, and we set off along the river. I carry the loaded sawn-off scatter gun across the saddle in front of me in case we scare up some game.

It's a beautiful morning for traveling, with the river nearby and the air warming in the rising sun. However, after a couple of hours the river turns north and we turn south and are back once more in a broad dry valley. At least I have a pair of plump quail hanging from my saddle horn, so there'll be fresh meat for supper.

At first I don't realize that I have reached Esqueda. The outskirts are nothing more than abandoned adobe houses with collapsed roofs. Pigeons and crows fly through empty windows, and a skinny dog stares suspiciously at me from a gaping doorway. My hopes of replenishing my supplies and finding a bed for the night after a long day's ride vanish.

Eventually I come to buildings that are still inhabited. Skinny children in rags appear for a moment, their large eyes staring, and then vanish. I feel I am being watched from the doorways and windows but I see nothing except the occasional vague movement.

I have resigned myself to riding on to find a suitable campsite where I can roast the quail, when an old man steps out of a doorway. His black jacket is short, cut to his waist and decorated with tarnished silver buttons.

His pants are narrow and also black with silver braid decorating the seams. The man's white beard and hair are neatly trimmed.

"*Buenas tardes*," he greets me.

I rein in Coronado. "*Buenas tardes*," I reply. "*¿Está esto la ciudad de Esqueda?*"

"*Sí.*" The old man nods. "*¿Es usted americano?*"

"*No, señor. Soy de Canadá.*" I am speaking haltingly, struggling to understand his simple questions and make up answers that, I hope, aren't too bad. "Do you speak English?" I ask, hopefully.

"Oh yes, certainly," the old man says with a wide grin. "In my youth I worked for the Governor of Alta California in Monterey. It was my job to present the complaints of the Americano settlers to the governor. But I am being unforgivably rude. Please, you must come in and take some supper with us. I insist."

"I should be honored," I say, charmed by the old man. He seems like an island of civilization in this wilderness.

"Excellent. But before that, we must tend to your horse. A horse is everything in this land and must be well cared for."

Leading Coronado, I follow the old man around the back of the house. I notice that his right leg is shorter than his left, forcing him to walk with a pronounced limp. He gives me a brush, and I unsaddle Coronado and brush him down. Behind the house is a large courtyard surrounded by a low adobe wall. Down one side are a dozen roofed horse stalls. Only one is occupied by an ancient, skinny gray horse. As directed by the old man, I lead Coronado to the stall beside the gray, throw in an armful of hay, some grain and a bucket of water. "You'll have a comfortable night here," I whisper.

"My name is Luis Santiago de Borica," the old man says as he leads me back to the house. "Please to call me Santiago."

"My name is James Doolen," I say, "but I have been given a new name since I came down here: Busca."

"Busca, the seeker. And what is it you seek?"

"My father."

"A very worthy quest," Santiago says as he ushers me into his house.

The house is not big, but the rooms are airy and have high ceilings, giving the impression of coolness and space. The room we enter is the kitchen.

"It is not the governor's palace in Monterey," Santiago says with a shrug, "but it suits my needs nicely."

A small woman bustles through a side door. "Ah, Maria." The old man's face lights up with pleasure.

"Please meet our guest, James Doolen, known as Busca. Busca, this is my companion of half a century, Maria Ygnacia."

I step forward and shake Maria's hand. It feels tiny and birdlike.

"I'm honored to meet you, ma'am," I say, feeling a strange need to be very formal in the presence of this elegant old couple. "And I would be delighted if you would accept these as a token of my thanks for your hospitality to a traveler." I hand over the two quail.

"I am honored to meet you," Maria says as she executes a surprisingly delicate curtsey and sweeps the quail out of my hand. "I am certain the governor will look kindly upon your petition. Now, if you will excuse me, there is to be a banquet tonight and I must take these to the kitchens for preparation."

Maria scuttles over to the range and busies herself with the fire, leaving me standing openmouthed in confusion.

"Do not concern yourself," Santiago says. "The years have not dealt as kindly with my dear Maria as with me. As you saw, she sometimes returns in her head to the governor's palace in Monterey. It is a harmless confusion, and I assure you, she will do your gift proud. Now"—he places a hand on my back—

"let us sit and take the evening air over a glass of refreshment."

We return to the courtyard and sit on two barely serviceable chairs at a long, heavy oak table. Santiago disappears into the house and returns with a bottle half filled with a rich amber liquid, and two glasses.

"It is *mezcal de tequila*, a drink made from the juice of the agave plant."

Santiago pours measures of the liquid into two glasses and pushes one over to me. "*Salud*," he says, holding his glass up.

"*Salud*," I repeat, raising my glass to clink against his. Fortunately, I only take the daintiest of sips of the drink. The fiery liquid scorches my throat and begins a violent fit of coughing.

"My apologies," Santiago says as I calm down. "I did not know that you were unfamiliar with our local drink." He gazes thoughtfully at his glass. "It is true that it is not the fine French cognac I drank many years ago," he says ruefully, "but times change and we must change with them. But I would be honored if you would tell me the tale of your quest thus far."

I place the glass to one side on the table and launch into the story of my travels and the characters I have met. Santiago listens with quiet interest.

"You are a very dedicated young man," he says when I am done. "Would that more sons were as devoted to their parents. I thank you for sharing your tale. We do not receive much news of the outside world in our little backwater. With your permission, may I ask you a couple of questions?"

"Of course," I reply, but Santiago has no chance to frame his enquiries as Maria calls us in to eat.

he meal is the best I have had since I left home, well, most of it is. Maria has cut up the two quail and cooked them in a dark stew with several kinds of beans. The stew is spicy and has a strange, but not unpleasant, musky flavor that Maria tells me proudly is due to something called achiote seeds. We eat the stew with thick, warm tortillas, and when we are done, I regret not having twice as many quail with me.

My only mistake is taking a mouthful of the chopped green and red peppers that Santiago and Maria enthusiastically add to their tortillas. My mouth explodes into flames—at least that's how it feels—and I only manage to douse the flames with a mouthful of tortilla.

"My apologies," Santiago says as Maria looks on sympathetically. "I should have warned you that the small wild peppers, *tepins*, that grow hereabouts are quite hot. I do hope you do not think that we are attempting to poison you."

"No," I gasp. "I'm just not used to spicy food."

After we finish and Maria clears away, Santiago and I return outside where I politely refuse one of the long, thin cigars that my companion smokes with great enjoyment.

"What made you settle in Esqueda?" I ask.

"My family has roots here," Santiago explains. "My father was born and I spent my early childhood over the mountains in Casas Grandes." I start at the mention. Everywhere I look this name comes up, but I stay silent and let Santiago continue. "My father was killed in 1811 in Father Miguel Hidalgo y Costilla's revolt that began our war for independence from Spain.

"After that, my mother took me to Mexico City where she met and married a young diplomat. It was my stepfather's career that took us to Alta California and work with the governor. After California was lost to the Americans in the war of '47, Maria and I returned to Mexico. I tried to continue working in politics, but my heart wasn't in it. The corruption and self-interest saddened me, so we moved to Esqueda.

"The town was much more prosperous then, and there were well-tended ranches along the valley, but years of Apache raids and the visits of the scalp hunters drove many people to seek a life elsewhere. Maria and I are old now—sometimes I think I live in the past as much as my wife—and we have no children, so where would we go?"

Santiago gazes across the compound to where Coronado stands contentedly in his stall. Now I have another story to remember.

"Wellington taught me that stories are important," I say, "so thank you for sharing yours with me."

"*No es nada*," Santiago says. "Your name is Doolen, no?"

"It is," I say.

"And that is an Irish name?" he asks thoughtfully.

"Yes."

"It was your father's name?"

"Of course. Why do you ask?"

"Nothing. It is not a common name, that is all. May I ask you the questions I had in mind before Maria called us in to dinner?"

"Certainly."

"What makes you so sure you will find your father, or news of him, in Casas Grandes?"

"He left me a letter saying that he was going there. Of course, that was ten years ago, so who knows what happened."

"Indeed." Santiago strokes his chin. "And how old would your father be?"

I frown, puzzled by where these questions could be leading. "My mother said he would be forty-five this year."

"So that means," Santiago pauses, "that he was born in the year of 1832."

"Yes, I guess so. Why does this matter?"

"I just have one more question. Was there a name in this letter he wrote you?"

"Yes, Don Alfonso Ramirez. He has a hacienda…" My voice trails into silence as I see Santiago's reaction. His eyes close, his forehead drops into his hand and he lets out a long sigh. "What's the matter?" I ask.

With an obvious effort, he lifts his head and looks at me. "And you have no idea who this Alfonso Ramirez is?"

"Other than the mention in my father's letter, I know nothing about him. What does this mean? What's going on?"

"I'm not certain what it means, but I can give you some information that may help you in your quest."

"Then give it," I say eagerly.

"Perhaps once I tell you, you will regret your keenness to know, but the old man you met, Wellington, is correct; stories are important. And I suspect that what I am about to tell you may be a part of your story."

Santiago paused as if gathering himself before he continued.

"When I was a mere boy in Casas Grandes, there was a landowner named Ramirez who owned a ranch outside the town. His ranch was the largest for many miles around and he was immensely rich. His hacienda was a wonder to behold, filled with magnificent paintings and furniture from Europe. The floors were hardwoods from South America, and he had a library larger than the entire house Maria and I now live in. His stables were famous and filled with the finest Arabian breeding stock. Ranchers used to visit from all over New Spain—this was before our war for independence—to buy colts from his breeding line."

Santiago reached for his glass, which still sat on the table, poured some of the amber alcohol into it and took a drink. I struggled to hold myself under control and not shout at him to tell me what he knew.

"With all he possessed, this Ramirez should have been happy, but he was not. It was said that he beat the workers in his fields and his young wife as readily as he beat his horses. But he was rich and powerful. He was the law around Casas Grandes, so no one could do anything to stop him. My father was the only one who tried.

"After Ramirez beat a worker to death, my father rode the two hundred miles to the state capital of Chihuahua and lodged a formal disposition of complaint, charging Ramirez with murder. My father was correct in what he did, but he was naïve. The judges to whom he complained were all rich landowners and friends of Ramirez. They listened to my father politely but did nothing. The only consequence of my father's brave action was that he earned Ramirez's undying hatred.

"When Father Hidalgo raised the banner of rebellion against Spain in 1810, my father was overjoyed. Although I was only a boy of eleven, I vividly remember him sitting me on his knee and telling me that this was a new dawn. That freedom from Spain would mean freedom for everyone from the likes of Ramirez."

Santiago smiles ruefully. "Again he was naïve. Hidalgo's army was defeated and the survivors fled north.

Hidalgo was betrayed; some say that Ramirez was involved, but, in any case, Father Hidalgo and his companions were taken to Chihuahua for trial. My father, although heartbroken at the defeat of his dreams, insisted on traveling to Chihuahua to see his heroes. While he was there, Ramirez denounced him as a revolutionary traitor to the very judges my father had spoken with only a few months before. Without any evidence they accepted Ramirez's charge, and my father was sentenced to be executed.

"My father was shot the day before Hidalgo, July 29, 1811, my twelfth birthday. His head was cut off and placed in an iron cage and hung from the gate of Ramirez's hacienda as a warning to others. Of course, my mother was in an impossible position, and that is when we fled to Mexico City to begin a new life."

Santiago takes another drink and gazes thoughtfully into his glass. I sit in confusion. It is a sad story, but what does it have to do with me?

"Was he the Don Alfonso Ramirez in my father's letter?"

Santiago looks startled, as if he has forgotten my presence. "No. No," he says. "I am sorry. My mind tends to wander these days. The Ramirez in this story died many years ago, but he had a son. A boy of my age, called Alfonso.

"After my father was killed and before we left for Mexico City, I used to visit the gates of the Ramirez hacienda, where they had hung my father's head."

Santiago notices the look of shock that crosses my face.

"I know," he says, smiling ruefully, "it is a gruesome thing for a twelve-year-old boy to visit the severed head of his father, but those were violent times and there was no grave for me to visit.

"I used to talk to my father's head as it swung gently in its iron cage above the gate. I would tell him how mother was doing, about our plans to move to Mexico City and about my dreams of avenging his death.

"One day as I stood before the gates, Alfonso Ramirez returned from a hunting trip with two companions. I moved aside to let them pass, but Alfonso reined in and addressed me. 'So you are the son of the traitor hanging from our gate. I have heard that you come to visit him. Does he enjoy the visits?'

"Alfonso's companions laughed coarsely, but I remained silent. 'I asked you a question and I expect an answer. Are we not generous? Aren't you glad we hung your traitor father's head from our gate so that you could come and have these enlightening conversations with it?'

"Anger boiled in me, but I pushed it back. I could not fight three mounted men. I turned and walked away.

"I heard the hoofbeats and half turned before Alfonso rode me down. I think my leg broke that first time, but Alfonso didn't stop. I lay in a haze of hooves and pain, protecting my head as best I could as he rode back and forth over me. All the while, Alfonso was shouting, 'This is how we teach peasants to respect us,' and his companions were laughing.

"Eventually the nightmare stopped, and they left me for dead. I was bruised and bleeding everywhere and several ribs were broken. My left arm and right leg were also broken. I couldn't move. I could barely breathe for the pain.

"Luckily, a woodcutter found me and took me home. It took many months but my injuries finally healed, all except my leg, which set crooked and has blessed me with this limp all my life. As soon as I was well enough to travel, we moved to Mexico City."

Santiago pours himself another drink and drains his glass as if he needs the alcohol to push back the memories of that day. I'm shocked by what he tells me but still confused as to what it has to do with me. At last, Santiago feels up to going on.

"I never returned to Casas Grandes or exacted the revenge I had promised my father I would. However, as I prospered, I kept myself informed of Alfonso Ramirez's life. His father died in a riding accident in 1821, the year Mexico finally achieved independence from Spain.

"Alfonso inherited the ranch, prospered and developed a reputation for cruelty that surpassed even his father's. Although only in his early twenties, he became obsessed with having a son to follow him and set about searching for a suitable wife. Through his network of powerful connections, he soon found one, a young immigrant girl called Maeve. I can only assume that she was swept off her feet by visions of Alfonso's wealth and power.

"In any case, the son that Alfonso craved did not arrive. For ten years, the couple remained barren. There were births, but the infants were either stillborn or sickly and died soon after birth. I shudder sometimes when I think what the poor girl's life must have been like in that decade, no better than a slave to Alfonso's desire for a son. I do not for a moment imagine that Alfonso was capable of doing anything other than blaming her for the lack of an heir, and his blame was not something any person would wish to draw upon themselves.

"Eventually, though, Maeve became pregnant once more and bore a healthy son. Alfonso was ecstatic, but it had been a very exhausting birth, and that night Maeve began bleeding. Alfonso was celebrating, drinking and showing off his son to his cronies. He ignored Maeve's problems and the midwife's pleas that the doctor be fetched.

"That night, Maeve died. It is said that, when he was told the news, Alfonso merely finished his drink and said, 'It is of no consequence. She has given me a son.'

"The son, Roberto, grew strong and—"

"Roberto Ramirez was the famous scalp hunter," I interrupt.

Santiago nods. "That is what some say, although so many stories have grown up around him now, that it is impossible to separate fact from fiction. He carried the burden of his father's evil reputation around on his back like a stone.

"What is certain is that Roberto did not turn out to be the son that Alfonso craved. Before he reached the age of ten, he ran off into the desert one night and never returned. When Alfonso was told that his son had gone, he flew into a rage and beat the messenger to death with his bare hands.

"By then, Alfonso had married once more, a Mexican woman, and she had born him a second son, a couple of years after Roberto was born. Alfonso now had two sons, but, so the story goes, Roberto was the only one he ever cared for."

"Is Alfonso Ramirez still alive?"

"No. He died almost thirty years ago, at the time when the scalp hunters were so busy. The last years of Alfonso's life were not happy. He became more cruel than ever, driving the workers away and letting the ranch and hacienda run down. His wife died—I do not know the circumstances—and Apache attacks drove off most of Alfonso's fine horses and what workers had stayed with him. In the end, only his second son stayed beside him, so I suppose he at least got his wish for a loyal son."

Santiago falls silent. It's an incredible tale of violence and death, but I am still confused.

"Thank you for telling me this," I say. "It fills in gaps in what I have heard, but what does it have to do with my father?"

"I'm not certain," Santiago says. "I never saw Alfonso's first wife, Maeve, or any of his family for that matter. She was said to be a great beauty and very charming with dark hair, flashing eyes and the wit of her ancestors. You see, Maeve came from Ireland and her family name was Doolen."

12

I've been riding east through the mountains and thinking about what Santiago told me every waking moment for the two days since I left Esqueda. I can come up with only two possibilities for what it all means. Either it means nothing—Alfonso Ramirez's first wife had the same name as my father by coincidence—or Maeve Doolen was in some way related to my father, and hence me.

A coincidence, given that my father mentioned both Casas Grandes and Alfonso Ramirez in his letter, seems remote in the extreme. The name Ramirez and the town of Casas Grandes are inextricably linked with my past and that suggests strongly that the tragic Maeve Doolen is as well.

So, if there is a connection, what can it be? Maeve married Alfonso very soon after Mexico gained independence in 1821, which would make her around thirty years older than my father, so it seems unlikely that they were brother and sister. Perhaps, my father is the son of Maeve's brother, which would make her his aunt and my great-aunt. It seems plausible given that Irish families were probably quite large. At least now I know to ask about the Doolen name when I reach Casas Grandes.

What makes me shudder is the thought that the foul Alfonso Ramirez might have been my great-uncle and his son, the scalp hunter Roberto, my cousin!

I ride on, running the same thoughts round and round my brain without getting anywhere. The trail has been climbing steadily since I left Esqueda, and now I am deep in the mountains. There is a blanket of old snow on the ground, and Coronado and I exhale clouds of white breath in the cold air. I have my blanket wrapped tightly around me and hope that Santiago's information—that we should cross the pass this afternoon and be able to descend the other side before nightfall—is correct.

Once over the mountains the journey should be easier. Casas Grandes will still be several days away, but we will be traveling along valleys in a huge arc around the north end of the next mountain range. At the moment, we are working our way around the shoulder of a mountain, and I hope the pass will come into view soon. Fortunately, the snow is old and the trail is marked by the tracks of those who have already passed this way.

———— ◆ ————

At first I think that the bloody patches on the snow below the pass are where some hunters have butchered their game. I am right about hunters and butchering, but the game is human.

The first body is sprawled beside the trail, arms spread out as if pleading for help. It is an Apache warrior, killed by a bullet through the chest. The top of his head is a bloody mess, and there are marks in the snow where someone sat, as Ed had described to me, hauling off the man's scalp.

In all, I count five bodies, two quite far from the trail where they ran to try and escape or find some cover from which to fight back. Most have been shot, but some show ax or knife cuts. All have been scalped.

The last one lies almost at the summit of the pass, and, horrifically, he was still alive after he was scalped. I can see the bloodstained trail where he dragged himself along before he finally expired.

I cross the pass, deep in thought. It was obviously an ambush. The party of Apaches were fired on without warning from rocks higher up the mountainside. Their ponies and weapons are gone, but obviously the reason for the massacre was to acquire scalps. Is someone still paying for such gruesome human trophies?

After a while, I notice that there are splashes of blood on the snow beside the trail. Does this mean that one or more of the victims escaped?

———◆———

By dusk, the trail has descended far enough that there are only patches of dirty snow in sheltered hollows. I move off into the scrub trees to one side, find a small, relatively flat open area and make camp. I have brushed down Coronado with the brush Santiago gave me, tethered him, collected a decent pile of firewood and warmed myself by a good blaze when I sense someone behind me. Before I can turn, a strong arm wraps itself around my neck and a knife blade, glinting in the fire-light, wavers before my eyes.

"Do not struggle, Busca," a familiar voice says in my ear. "It is Nah-kee-tats-an, and it would be bad luck to kill you."

The arm releases me and I turn. The Apache warrior who confronted me on the trail days ago is crouching beside me. His left hand holds his knife, but it is low and the shoulder of his shirt is soaked in blood.

"You're wounded," I say, realizing that he is the survivor of the massacre who left the blood splashes by the trail.

"It is not much," he says. "Only enough to remind me of my dead friends when I find the men who killed them."

"Who was it?"

"Scalp hunters. Three warriors fell dead, and I was wounded in the first volley. Two tried to fight back, but there was no cover and they were cut down. Their death gave me my chance to escape over the pass. I was hiding here awaiting dark when you arrived. My father was right; I will not die easily a second time.

"And you, Busca, you are twice lucky. I thought at first you were one of them. I was ready once more to kill you."

"Thank you for not killing me," I say weakly. "I have a little food. Will you join me by the fire?"

"I would be honored, Busca."

"Where were you headed when you were attacked?" I ask after I have shared out the last of the tortillas and beans that Santiago gave me.

Nah-kee-tats-an thinks for a long minute before answering. "We were going to join Victorio, who is collecting a band in the mountains to the east. Tell me, Busca. How were the bodies of my companions?"

It takes me a moment to work out what the question means. "They were scalped," I reply eventually.

Nah-kee-tats-an nods. "As I thought. It is the old days that Too-ah-yay-say talks of returned."

"Roberto Ramirez and the scalp hunters?" I ask without thinking. What would this proud man think if he knew that I suspected I was related to the worst of the scalp hunters?

"There is a story my people tell of this Ramirez," Nah-kee-tats-an says. "One day, some women found a child wandering in the desert. He was lost and near death. They took him back to their village and cared for him until he regained his strength. He said his name was Ramirez, and he lived with my people for many years.

"One day, a party of scalp hunters attacked the village while the men were away on a raid. Ramirez organized the boys of the village to defend the women and infants. They fought bravely, surprising the scalp hunters with their violence. However, they were being pushed back on all sides when the men returned. The scalp hunters were defeated and fled, leaving several bodies around the village. While the people tended their wounds and celebrated their deliverance, the Ramirez boy was found going around the bodies, slitting the throats of those who showed any signs of life and scalping the bodies. As a reward for his bravery, the warriors allowed him to keep the scalps and he became a respected member of the band.

"But the old ways were vanishing. The people were hunted and spent their lives fleeing from hideout to hideout. Eventually, when there were but a handful left, Ramirez disappeared. He took with him the scalps that he had been given in the scalp hunter's raid."

Nah-kee-tats-an fell silent. I am about to ask if knows any stories about Roberto Ramirez after that, but he abruptly stands up and says, "I must tend to my pony," and disappears into the trees.

I sit and try to make sense of the many pieces of information I have collected about Roberto Ramirez.

Ed dismissed him as the most brutal of the scalp hunters. Wellington suggested that any story about him depended on who told it. Nah-kee-tats-an's story fitted with what Santiago had told me of Alfonso's son running away from home as a boy, but the boy adopted into an Apache band for helping fight off the scalp hunters didn't sound like someone who would turn into one of the very people he had fought against.

My head swirls with all the stories I've been told. They are all different, but bits of all of them talk of the Ramirez clan, Casas Grandes and scalp hunters. Perhaps they are all part of one story: mine. It's confusing, but I am determined to continue and find out everything I can.

Unfortunately, I don't get a chance to find out any more from Nah-kee-tats-an. After he returns from tending his horse, he lies down without a word and falls asleep. When I awake the next morning, he's gone.

As far as I can see, ruined adobe walls, some thirty or forty feet high, rise as if growing from the brown desert floor. Green and blue lizards scuttle up walls, and swallows swoop through empty windows far above my head. The black stumps of beams jut from walls where long-collapsed floors once spanned rooms, and thick growths of cactus block doorways that lead nowhere.

It's almost impossible to imagine these barren squares bustling with vendors selling brightly colored cloth, painted pots and exotic birds, or to see laughing children chasing each other through these long-abandoned courtyards and rooms. Yet this place must once have been a thriving city at least as big as San Diego.

Casas Grandes is a city of the ancients Wellington told me about, a city that was a ruin long before even the Apaches arrived in this land. A city that may have spawned the legend of the city of gold that drew Coronado on in his unsuccessful search. But if this is a city of the ancients, where is the modern town and Alfonso Ramirez's hacienda?

I ride on, eventually leaving the ruins behind, and arrive at a place that is filled with more than ghosts. Modern Casas Grandes is a pale shadow of what the ancient city must have been, but at least there are people here. They watch me warily as I pass.

I ride down the main street and come to a saloon. It's a low adobe building with a dark doorway. It's not at all inviting, but there are five horses tethered outside, suggesting that it is occupied and might be a good place to ask about the Ramirez hacienda or if anyone remembers the name Doolen.

As I dismount, a man steps out of the nearby alley. He's skinny, with high cheekbones, a sharp nose and sallow skin. His hair is long and greasy and he wears a mustache and chin beard. His eyes are an unsettling shade of blue, and there's no friendship in them as they scan me and Coronado.

"Howdy," the man says. "You planning on stopping to wet your whistle?"

"I am," I reply, although part of me is regretting not just riding on.

The thin man lets me go ahead. As we head for the doorway, I examine the dust-covered horses. They're a mixed bunch, but all are lean and their tack worn. The last one in line makes me hesitate. It's a large black horse, and there are a cluster of fresh scalps and one old one hanging from the saddle horn. The horn itself is ornamented with some worn silver work.

I only have time to register all this before the stranger grabs me by the shoulders and shoves me violently into the darkened barroom. I stumble painfully against a table. Four figures standing at the crude bar turn and stare at the commotion. As my eyes adjust to the gloom, I see that the figure nearest me is Ed.

"Well, look who it is," he says. "Maybe Red and the Kid were right and we should have killed you back outside Tucson."

"He come in riding the Kid's horse," the thin man says.

"Is that so?" Ed steps forward and stares at me with interest. "Now, we know what happened to Red— he got careless and his hair's hanging off some savage's war lance—but the Kid, he'd be a mystery. Last I seen of him, he was getting drunk on your money in Tucson, telling me that he'd catch us up the next day. Ain't seen him since. I don't suppose you could shed any light on what might've happened to him?"

I stay silent and Ed steps forward and punches me hard on the cheek. I stagger back, but the thin man grabs me and pushes me back toward Ed.

"I saved your life once," Ed says. "Don't think it's gonna happen again. The Kid's missing and you come riding in here on his horse. You'd better start talking if you want to leave this room alive, and I don't want any fanciful tales of finding the horse wandering in the desert."

"An old Apache gave him to me."

Ed hits me again. "I thought I was clear about not wanting to hear any fanciful tales. Slim," Ed addresses the thin man behind me, "take him outside and shoot him."

"Sure," Slim says, grabbing me by the arm.

"Wait!" I yell. "I'll tell you what happened."

"That's better," Ed says with a smile, "but make it snappy and convincing. Slim ain't known for his patience."

"I saw the Kid in Tucson the day after you robbed me. I went out on the trail to ambush him. I didn't plan to kill him, just force him to give me my stuff back, but he was drunk. He shot at me—that's where I got these cuts on my cheek—and I shot back. I don't know if my bullet killed him, but he fell off his horse and smashed his head on a rock."

"And you took his horse?"

"No. The horse ran off. I buried the Kid as best I could. I was found by an old Apache who lives in a cave in the hills. He found the Kid's horse and gave him to me."

Ed tilts his head and regards me with interest. "That sounds more like the truth. The Kid never could hold his liquor worth a damn."

"Can I kill him now?" Slim asks over my shoulder.

"Not just yet," Ed says to my great relief. "Me and young Jim Doolen have got ourselves some history, and there's a place we need to go and something I need to tell him before you can have your fun. Tie him up, put him on the Kid's horse and let's move out."

We ride out of town with Ed holding Coronado's reins and me desperately trying to stay on the horse's back. My hands are tied, and Coronado seems extremely skittish, dancing from one side to the other and tossing his head up and down. I talk to him to try and calm him down, but it does no good. He simply doesn't like being in the company of Ed and the others. I know how he feels.

Fortunately the ride is short, and we soon arrive at a crumbling adobe arch. A single ornate rusted gate hangs at a crazy angle off a bent hinge. I look up and wonder if the rusted hook on the peak of the arch is where Santiago's father's head hung.

"You boys wait here," Ed orders. "We won't be long."

"Don't forget your promise," Slim says, sending a shiver down my spine.

Ed leads the way through the gateway and along a curving path toward a long low building. The main part, I assume the house itself, is fronted by a wide verandah, the roof of which is supported by a series of elegant adobe pillars and arches. In the center there is a broader arch that leads to a wide doorway. To each side are less elegant buildings that were once probably bunkhouses, storerooms and stables. The whole impressive complex is bathed in a soft orange glow as the sun lowers toward the western horizon.

Ed rides straight at the building, up the two stone steps onto the verandah and through the doors into the main hallway. Coronado is forced to follow but is restless, and his hooves clatter on the dark stone floor.

Once in the room, Ed wheels his horse and drops Coronado's reins. I briefly consider making a run for it, but even if I manage to stay on Coronado's back with my hands tied, I would be caught in minutes.

"Do you know where we are?" Ed asks me.

"Alfonso Ramirez's hacienda?" I guess.

"Right. Look around."

The room has obviously been abandoned for a long time. There is a large hole in the roof at one end and a pile of broken wooden beams, adobe bricks and tiles beneath it. The mud nests of swallows are everywhere and several of the birds swoop and dive in annoyance at being disturbed. The walls are bare and the plaster, which shows the remnants of red and blue painted patterns on it, is peeling and chipped. The floor, made of some polished black stone, is covered in a layer of dust and tiny sand dunes that have blown in through the open door.

"The kitchens are through that doorway." Ed points to a gap in the wall beside the large empty fireplace at one end of the room. "Alfonso took great pride in his ability to entertain. There was an oak table that ran the entire length of the room and, on feast days, a continuous line of servants coming through from the kitchens, bringing food and drink for the guests. Often there would be a guitarist or two at the opposite end, playing traditional Spanish songs."

I've stopped looking around the room and am staring at Ed.

"You can't imagine what it was like, the sound of the crackling fire, the clinking glasses and cutlery, the music, the chatter. It was magical."

"How do you know all this?" I ask, my brow furrowing.

Ed tears himself back from his reminiscences and looks at me. He speaks slowly. "I know all this because I grew up here. When we met before, I told you that Ed was short for Eduardo, but I never told you my surname. It is Ramirez. Alfonso was my father, and I was born in 1834 in a room through that door." He waves an arm at a doorway at the opposite end of the room from the fireplace.

My mind flashes back to the story Santiago told me. Alfonso married twice and had a second son a couple of years younger than Roberto.

"Roberto Ramirez is your brother," I say.

"Half brother," Ed acknowledges, "and was. He died near ten years ago, quite close to where I met you, as it happens."

My mind reels with questions, but before I can get any out, Ed continues.

"But that ain't the beginning of the story. It starts when I was sixteen years old and I discovered that my brother was still alive."

"**R**oberto ran off when I was no more'n seven or eight. Alfonso flew into a wild rage when he heard and beat the servant who told him the news to death before my eyes. After that, Roberto's name was never mentioned. He was dead to all of us. It was fine by me. Roberto had always been my father's favorite and I hated him. I was happy he was dead and looked forward to Alfonso now treating me as he had Roberto."

As he speaks, I realize that Ed has changed. Gone is the coarse language of the cowboy that he used with his gang. Replacing it are the cultured tones of a Mexican landowner that he let me glimpse outside Tucson. He reminds me of those lizards in Africa that can change color to fit in with their background. As a bushwhacker on the trail or a scalp hunter with his gang, he is as rough as needs be. In the ruined hall of his father's hacienda, he reverts to an older persona. I wonder how many other masks he has worn in his complex and violent life.

"Didn't work out that way. Even dead, Roberto was still my father's favorite son." The bitterness in Ed's voice sends shivers through me. "I lived every moment of my life trying to please Alfonso. Trying to be Roberto. It was no use; never once did my father show me the slightest affection. Oh, he spent time with me, taught me how to shoot and use a knife, but it was like he was training a horse; there was no passion or reward in it, no sugar cube when I got things right, just beatings when I got something wrong."

Ed smiles ruefully. "Alfonso was always telling me, 'Life's hard. There's always someone out to get you; if it's not Apaches after your scalp, it's a neighbor wants to steal your land or some revolutionary wants your power. The only way to survive is to be faster and harder than them. Hit them before they can hit you and don't ever let them close to you. Once you start to care about someone, you have a weakness and they'll exploit it.'

"I grew up believing that, but I reckon I'm getting soft in my old age. I stopped the Kid from killing you and now the Kid's dead and here you are causing me difficulties again. I won't make the same mistake twice."

I shudder at that last statement, but there's nothing I can do but listen to the rest of his tale. This is where my quest has led me and, for all my fear, I must listen to this final story.

"I think Alfonso went mad after my mother died of the fever. He would walk around the hacienda at night, calling Roberto's name and weeping. He let the ranch fall away and would beat the servants at the least excuse. They began to call him *loco*, and more and more of them would disappear in the night. Apache attacks drove the rest away. Eventually it was just him and me. I thought about leaving too, but surely, if I was all he had left, he would begin to treat me with the respect I craved.

"When I was sixteen, Roberto came home. I was outside skinning a jackrabbit I had just shot when I heard shouting from the house. I ran in and saw Alfonso standing over there." Ed waves his hand toward the fireplace. "There was a stranger standing facing him, holding a small pistol in his right hand. He wore his hair long in the Apache fashion, but he was dressed in cowboy clothes. They stood about a foot apart and were too engrossed in their argument to notice me.

"'I should kill you now,' the stranger said. 'I returned to resolve things between us, but I talked to the townspeople and they told me what happened the night of my birth. You let her die.'

"'She would have died anyway,' Alfonso said in a voice that was so cold it scared me. 'Anyway, you were what was important, the next generation, a son to take over the ranch, to give me immortality. You had responsibilities. Instead, what do you do? You shame me by running off to live like a savage. Now, all these years later, you crawl back whining about resolving things. I'm glad your mother died. She was weak, and you've inherited that weakness. All you are worth is the money I could get for your scalp.'

"I was confused," Ed went on, "but I was gradually realizing who this must be. The stranger cocked his pistol and raised it to point into Alfonso's face. His hand was shaking.

"'Go on,' Alfonso sneered. 'Shoot me. It would be the one real thing you have ever done.'

"For a moment I was frozen in terror, thinking that this man was going to kill my father. Strangely, even in my confusion, all I could think of was saving my father's life.

Perhaps then he would care for me. The stranger let out a long sigh and lowered his weapon. I made a run at him just as Alfonso made a grab for the pistol. The three of us twisted around. Then the pistol went off.

"The stranger jumped back, pulling me with him. My father stood alone with a frown on his face. He was staring down at the left side of his stomach and his hands were held out in front of him in an almost pleading gesture. A wisp of smoke was rising slowly from a burned circle on his shirt and dark blood was already beginning to well out of a black hole at the center of the circle.

"'You killed me,' Alfonso said and took an unsteady step forward. He looked up at the stranger and spat full in his face. 'Damn you to hell,' he said and fell heavily forward against the corner of the oak table.

"The stranger said, 'Oh my god,' and stepped back, Alfonso's spit sliding down his cheek. He stared at my father, slumped in a crouch by the table, blood dripping into a growing puddle on the floor, and then he looked at me. For a moment, I thought he was going to shoot me too, but his expression was one of terrible sadness. Then he turned and fled."

Ed sits in silence on his horse, staring at the floor as if Alfonso's blood were still there. I don't think now that I could flee, even if I was't bound. I am beginning to suspect some of the places Ed's tale is taking me, and I feel as if I am standing on the edge of a precipice, my past yawning before me.

Eventually Ed continues. "I carried Alfonso to bed and tended him as best I could, but there was little I could do; the wound was fatal. It took my father five full days to die, most of it screaming in agony. I sat by his bed because I didn't know what else to do.

"The night he died, I was sleeping in a chair by his bedside. Something woke me and I looked up to see Alfonso sitting up. His face was thin and drawn and his sunken eyes gleamed with a feverish unnatural light. 'The man who shot me,' he said. 'His name was Roberto Ramirez. He is your half brother.'

"I had already worked out who the stranger was, but hearing that he was my half brother surprised me. My father had never told me he had been married before and I had assumed that Roberto and I had the same mother. I tried to talk, but Alfonso silenced me. 'I don't have much time. You must listen. I was married before, when I was a young man, to a foreign girl. Her name was Maeve Doolen. It was a mistake. She was weaker than me and life in this land requires strength.

"'She bore me Roberto; however, she did not have the will to survive and died the same night. From his earliest days, I saw that Roberto had inherited her weakness, so I worked to build his strength. As soon as he could walk, I forced him to ride, shoot, rope calves and work hard from dawn to dusk. He hated the life and wanted nothing more than to waste his time in books and daydreams, but I kept at it. To crush the weakness in Roberto, I beat him for the least infraction. To make him hard, I had to be hard.'

"Alfonso suddenly clenched his fists and grimaced as a wave of agony swept over him. Beads of sweat formed on his face and he gasped, but he fought the pain back and went on. 'I failed. Roberto would rather flee than face up to his responsibilities. I disowned him, tried to forget him. Of course, I had you, but you were not the first born and, for all his weaknesses, I never felt for you the way I did for Roberto.'"

I have the strongest feeling that Ed is about to cry, and I almost feel real sympathy for the tortured, unloved boy he had been. But he takes a deep breath and continues.

"I should have hated Alfonso then, but I couldn't. I still craved his blessing, so I sat and listened to the rest of his tale. 'I lived in hope that Roberto would come back and that we could be reconciled. As you saw, he returned, but only to torment me, to blame me for everything and tell me of some mad plan to go off looking for gold in California. You saw what happened.'

"I was weeping by now. It was obvious even to me that Alfonso was dying and the mad look in his eyes frightened me. He raised his hand to try and hit me, but he didn't have the strength. 'Don't be a weakling like your brother. You are the head of the family now. I do not care what you do with what is left of the ranch or your life. I have only one request of you. Roberto disgraced me, the family and you. That cannot be allowed. I want you to find him and kill him.'

"I suppose I must have gasped or looked shocked, because Alfonso suddenly reached forward and grabbed my shirt in his clawed hand. His dying face was inches away from mine. I could feel the spittle on my cheek as he spoke and see the empty depth in his eyes.

"'You must do this,' he said. 'It is an order, my dying wish. My honor and yours depend upon it. Swear an oath that you will do it or, by all that is holy, I will return from the grave and my ghost will haunt you into madness and death. Swear an oath!'

"I was utterly terrified. I didn't know what I was saying, I just did what he wanted. I swore an oath that I would search out and kill my brother."

For a moment, Ed looks like a helpless child. How could he have possibly grown into a normal person after an upbringing like that? But his face hardens. He takes his disgusting good-luck charm off his saddle horn and holds it up before me.

"D'you know what this is?"

"It's a scalp," I say, confused. "You told me."

"But whose?" There's a madness in Ed's eyes now. I shrug and he laughs crazily. "This," he says in a terrifyingly soft voice as he waves the hair slowly in front of my nose, "this is Alfonso Ramirez's scalp."

"Your father?" I gasp.

Ed laughs again. "For several weeks I lived alone in the ruins of the ranch as Alfonso's body slowly decayed and dried. I was haunted by nightmares in which he returned and reminded me of my promise. Eventually I decided I would have to keep my oath. I took his scalp with me so that he would know I had done it and not haunt me.

"I buried what was left of him and went searching for Roberto. I scoured all northern Mexico, but I was too late; he had done as he had told my father and gone to the California goldfields. I tried to convince myself that I had done my duty, so I didn't follow him, but the dreams didn't stop. I tried to kill Roberto in a different way. I got a band together, and for a couple of years in the early fifties when no one was too picky about where a scalp came from, we made good money."

"I thought Roberto rode as a scalp hunter in those years," I say in confusion.

"No," Ed says with a smile. "He was in California living under a false name. I figured if I couldn't kill his body, I could at least kill his name. For those years, I was Roberto Ramirez."

I stare at Ed in shock. "You used your brother's name?"

"I did and it made me free. I could do whatever I wanted, and everyone thought it was Roberto. While I was scalping women and children, it wasn't really me doing it, it was my damned brother. Finally, I was showing my father that I was better than Roberto."

The mad look hasn't left Ed's eyes as he tells me this. I'm scared, but there's nothing I can do but wait for him to go on with his story. Eventually he does.

"Through the fifties and sixties I moved around, scalping when there was money in it, rustling cattle up Lincoln County way, shooting buffalo for the army, robbing any travelers I fell in with, and always making sure that everyone knew it was Roberto Ramirez doing this. Problem was, I was free to do anything I wanted during the days, but the nights were bad. In my dreams Alfonso kept urging me to fulfill my oath. I even went out to California to try and find the real Roberto. I had no luck, although I did find a man who'd been his partner in the goldfields. The man said he'd moved on, following the gold."

The scalp hangs by his side, and his gaze drops to the floor. I am confused as to why Ed is telling me this. "Did you ever catch up with your brother?" I ask.

Ed's head snaps round as if I have hit him. His eyes stare at me coldly. "My story's not done yet and there's something I haven't told you. Something you need to know to understand the end."

Ed's gaze drifts away, and I think I am going to have to wait through another of his long silences, but he keeps talking, although his voice drops to near a whisper.

"When my brother went to California, I took his name, but he changed his as well. I don't know whether it was because he was ashamed of Ramirez or because Mexicans weren't looked on too kindly in the gold-fields. In any case, he took his mother's name. Roberto Ramirez became Bob Doolen."

The real Roberto Ramirez was my father. The cruel Don Alfonso Ramirez was my grandfather. The tragic Maeve Doolen was my grandmother. Ed is my uncle. My mouth hangs open in shock as I absorb the implications of what I have been told.

"What do you mean?" I ask stupidly.

"Just what I say."

"But what…?" I begin asking a question and then tail off, not knowing what to ask. A thought strikes me as I run through what this all means. "Were you waiting for me on the road when we first met?"

Ed smiles. "Smart kid. There's not many lone

travelers your age passing through Yuma, and you were easy to follow."

"How did you know I'd be passing through?"

Ed's smile broadens. "I still keep contacts here in Casas Grandes. Your letter to Don Alfonso Ramirez got to me. I was going to reply, but your second letter saying you were coming down arrived before I could. It was a simple matter to work out about when you'd arrive and sit and wait in Yuma. You even look a bit like your father, and after five minutes' talk, I was certain."

"But why didn't you say who you were, who I was? Why did you set up the ambush and rob me?"

"I reckon old habits die hard, and I weren't looking for a family reunion. I just wanted to see what you looked like. I stopped the Kid from killing you, and if you'd just gone on your way after that, like I suggested, none of this would've happened."

"I couldn't. I had to find out what it all meant."

Ed nods. "I should've known that. Stubbornness is a Ramirez trait, I guess."

The mention of the Ramirez name reminds me of why I am here. "Where's my father?"

"Well now. That's the final piece of the story. After I looked unsuccessfully for Roberto—Bob, I reckon we should call him now—in California, I gave up.

Decided I would just have to live with my nightmares and make the best of it. I come back to Arizona Territory and made do. War came along and that provided some opportunities for the likes of me. Then, winter of sixty-seven, I was having a drink in a bar in Tucson and who should waltz in but Bob's old mining buddy from California. Recognizes me right off and comes over. Says he can tell me things if I buy him a drink, so I buy him a drink.

"Seems this man had drifted up to the Cariboo in British Columbia, following all the other fools who look for gold. Didn't find no gold, but who should he bump into in a stopping house in Yale but his old partner Bob Doolen. Fella told me Bob was settled there, all nice and cozy with a good wife and strapping son. That'd be you, I reckon.

"I tried to forget about the whole thing, but I couldn't. Alfonso wouldn't let me, and I had no excuse once I knew where he was. I thought about going up there, but then I had an idea. I wrote to Bob Doolen up in Yale as if I was Alfonso Ramirez. Said his bullet hadn't killed me, that I was an old man now who saw the error of his ways and wanted to resolve things before I died."

Ed stops and laughs harshly. The more cultured persona of the storyteller is slipping, the harsh mask of the brutal road agent and scalp hunter replacing it. "Seems like I've been all of my family at one time or another. Anyways, the fool fell for it. Wrote straight back saying he was hotfooting it down to see the old man. Just like I done with you, I went out to Yuma and waited. Sure enough, he comes through and I follow him for a couple of days while I decide what I'm going to do.

"My first scheme was to bushwhack him. Easy enough on this trail, but it weren't right. Not after all I'd gone through. I needed more, so I went into his camp one night. We sat and talked around the fire. He didn't recognize me at first, but the more I talked, the more I could see him beginning to wonder.

"Eventually I came clean, told him the whole story. You know what the idiot did then? He says he was glad I'd done it. Says family's important and he was glad that we'd met up at last. He even comes around the fire to shake my hand."

Ed is staring into the distance over my left shoulder as if he's seeing the ten-year-old scene again. I can barely breathe. Everything I have done, every story I have heard, has been building to this moment.

"What happened?" I whisper hoarsely.

Ed's gaze flicks back to the present and my face.

"I shot him," he says matter-of-factly. "Didn't kill him right away; it took a second shot for that. He didn't even have a gun with him. Buried his body up on one of those ridges outside Tucson."

Ed's calm tone of voice and simple telling is more shocking than if he had screamed what had happened at me or broken down in tears. My father is dead, killed by this man before me, his own brother and my uncle.

A wave of rage sweeps over me, and I spur Coronado at Ed. The move takes him by surprise and our two horses clash violently. He struggles to control his mount, but my hands are tied. As Coronado rears and bucks, my rolled blanket is torn off the saddle and I fall, landing heavily on the stone floor. All the wind is knocked from me and I lie helpless, gasping painfully for breath. Ed regains control of his horse and stares down at me.

"At least you fought back," he says. "Maybe you're not as weak as your father. I'm sorry that you have to die, but I did give you a chance. And I can't be always looking over my shoulder to see if you might've decided on revenge. I should do it myself, but I did promise Slim that he could have you, so I guess this is goodbye."

Without another word, Ed turns his horse and trots through the doorway. Coronado stands undecided for a moment and then follows them out. Almost immediately, Slim's shape appears. He's carrying a huge wide-bladed knife in his right hand.

"Howdy," he says companionably as he steps forward.

Gasping for air, I scramble backward toward the fireplace.

"Ain't no place to go," Slim says. "You're mine now, and I aim to have me some fun."

In two strides, Slim is beside me and delivers a vicious kick to my ribs. He hits the still painful spot where the Kid kicked me, and I scream as shafts of pain course through me.

Slim places one knee painfully on my stomach and grabs my hair with his left hand, hauling my head up. "Now I've gotta decide how I'm gonna do this," he says with a smile. "You got pretty hair, so I'm wondering if'n I might just want to scalp you first. I'm told it don't hurt too much."

At first I think the shadow behind Slim is Ed come back to watch.

"Or I could take your eyes out first. I've heard it said that, if you pop them out careful, the eyeball hangs by a kind of thread but you can still see. Reckon I could pop one out, and you could look back on yourself. That'd be something not everyone—"

The knife slashes deeply across Slim's throat opening a gaping red wound. A look of surprise crosses the man's features and a jet of bright blood spurts from his neck. The blood feels warm on my face.

Slim drops his knife with a clatter and grabs at his neck. It does no good; the blood keeps coming. He gives a bubbling cough and falls to one side. I draw in a large breath and wince at the pain in my ribs.

Nah-kee-tats-an is standing over me, a bloody knife in one hand and a rifle over his shoulder.

"How did you get here?" I gasp.

Nah-kee-tats-an points toward the doorway that Ed said led to the kitchen and then places his finger to his lips. With one swift cut he slices through the ropes binding my hands. As I sit up and try to massage my wrists with my numb hands, he wipes his knife on his breeches and replaces it in the scabbard at his waist. Then he removes the rifle from his shoulder and leans over until his mouth is beside my ear. "Do you have a weapon?" he asks.

I glance over at my blanket lying on the other side of Slim's still-twitching body. In it are my pistol and the scatter gun. I nod. "I will shoot from the window through there." Nah-kee-tats-an gestures toward the kitchen.

"Kill anyone who comes through that door." He nods at the main entrance and slips away.

Slim is still now, his blue eyes open but looking at nothing. There is a surprisingly large pool of dark blood around his head.

"Slim," I hear Ed's voice from outside. "You gonna take all day? We need to make some miles."

Startled out of my shock by the sound, I scramble over Slim and claw at the bedroll. My fingers are sore and stiff as the blood fights its way back into them, but I manage to spread it out. Lying there are the scatter gun and the box containing my father's revolver. I try to undo the catch on the revolver box, but my fingers won't work properly. I hear the crash of a rifle shot from the next room, closely followed by a yell outside.

"What the hell?" I hear Ed shout and then the sound of feet running toward the door. I hear boots clatter on the stone porch, and there's a dark figure blocking the doorway. In one movement, I drop the box, grab the scatter gun, swing it up, cock the hammers and pull both triggers, praying that it's loaded.

The explosion deafens me and the kick of the gun knocks me over backward. Both barrels were loaded and the blast catches the figure square in the chest, hurling him backward onto the porch.

In a moment of unearthly silence, I watch the man's boots in the doorway kick a couple of times through the drifting gun smoke. Then the first bullet embeds itself in the back wall of the room, bringing down a shower of plaster fragments. Scooping up the revolver box in front of me, I scramble over and sit with my back to the wall between the doorway and the window. A hail of bullets fly through the openings, sending showers of plaster down all around. Trying to stay calm, I work on opening the box. Finally, the lid flies up and I grab the revolver.

I have four loaded chambers left from the time I shot the Kid. I doubt that, even if I have the time, my stiff fingers could load the other two. I make a quick calculation. There were five of them to begin with. Slim's dead and so's the man in the doorway. If I assume that Nah-kee-tats-an's shot counted, then that leaves two. Is one of them Ed? Yes, I heard his voice after Nah-kee-tats-an's shot.

I roll to one side and chance a quick glance out the corner of the window opening. I catch a glimpse of Ed aiming his Colt from behind a stone water trough. A shot comes from the kitchen, splashing water from the trough, but Ed doesn't flinch. There are horses milling about in confusion and the body of the man Nah-kee-tats-an shot lying to one side. There's one missing. I duck back down hurriedly as Ed fires.

"Ain't no need for this," Ed shouts at me. "Can you hear me, Jim?"

I stay silent.

"I admit to making a mistake sending Slim in," Ed continues after a while. "I acted too hurriedly, didn't think things through. I must be getting old.

"We're family, Jim. Ain't no way we should be trying to kill one another. I got a proposition. You come on out and you and me'll just ride away from here. Leave the past behind and head on up to Lincoln County. I hear there's good work to be had there. We'll be partners. How about that?"

Again I stay silent.

"Of course, we can't let that savage in there with you live, so you just put a bullet in him and walk on out here and we'll ride off. His scalp and the others I got will fetch a pretty penny and give us some traveling money. What d'you say?"

I look up to see Nah-kee-tats-an standing in the kitchen doorway. He's holding his rifle across his body and staring hard at me. He can't possibly think I'm going to do what Ed asks.

With lightning speed, Nah-kee-tats-an raises his rifle. "No," I yell and throw myself to one side. That's what saves my life, not from Nah-kee-tats-an's shot but from the bullet that comes from the opposite end of the room. I hear it crash into the wall beside me. I half roll and come up, pointing the revolver at the new threat, but there's no need. Ed's missing companion is kneeling in the opposite doorway, a pistol in his right hand pointing harmlessly at the ground and his left hand clawing ineffectually at the hole in his chest. As I watch, Nah-kee-tats-an fires again. The man's head jerks up and he collapses forward.

At first I think the next gunshot is the dead man's pistol going off as he falls, but it comes from behind me. I turn and bring my revolver up.

Nah-kee-tats-an is sitting in the kitchen doorway with his rifle lying across his lap and a spreading red stain on his chest. Ed is in the room, a smoking gun in his hand. He turns to look at me.

"Just us now," he says with a smile.

I hold the cocked revolver pointing squarely at his chest.

"No need for that," he says quietly. "I meant what I said about us being partners. There's been enough killing. Let's you and me stop it now."

He's right. There has been enough killing, not just here but through all the stories I've been told over the past days. Every tale I've been told has been filled with death: Perdido, the English hunter, Santiago's father, Maeve Doolen, Alfonso Ramirez, Nah-kee-tats-an's ambushed companions, and my father. I have come to this land to learn a story that is written in blood.

I look past Ed to see Nah-kee-tats-an sitting in the kitchen doorway. He's badly wounded, there is blood all down his right side, but he's still alive. His dark eyes are alert and fixed on me. He nods slowly.

I feel a rush of joy that he is alive. There has been too much death. Suddenly, my revolver feels incredibly heavy. My hand begins to sag. As it does, Ed's gun begins to come up.

"No!" I say, struggling to keep my revolver on Ed. "Please stop." My revolver's wavering.

"Come on now," Ed says gently as he continues to raise his gun, "you ain't gonna shoot me. We're family. I saved your life on the trail outside Tucson."

I grimace in confusion. Ed also put my life in danger, but can I kill him in cold blood? Suddenly, the image of my father leaps into my head. He's standing smiling at me. He's dressed for traveling and he's carrying a leather satchel over his shoulder.

You look after your Mom while I'm gone, he says and his smile broadens. *I'll have plenty more stories for you when I see you again. Remember the old sea captain in the book that never gave up looking for that whale, and keep practicing with that old revolver.* He winks at me and reaches forward to tousle my hair.

I feel anger building in me. My father never got the chance to tell me any more stories. Ed killed him.

I did what I was supposed to do. "I followed the clues you left," I say out loud. "Just like Ahab in *Moby Dick*. I kept going until I found out the whole story. It led me here."

"What?" Ed asks. His gun is rising with almost hypnotic slowness. I close my eyes and pull the trigger. Without looking, I cock the hammer and fire again, and again, and again. The fifth time there's nothing but a loud *click*. I let the revolver drop and open my eyes.

Ed is standing, his back against the doorjamb, watching me. His gun hangs limply by his side and he has a puzzled look on his face. Already, the front of his shirt is soaked in blood. His forehead wrinkles into a frown.

"We're family," he says. He tries to say more, but the blood gurgling up into his throat prevents him. Without taking his eyes off me, Ed slowly slides down the wall, leaving a bright red smear on the plaster. When he is sitting, he makes a final, feeble effort to raise his gun, but he's too weak. He shakes his head helplessly and slumps to the floor. By the time I crawl over to him, my uncle's dead.

Nah-kee-tats-an has lost a lot of blood, but his wound is clean. Ed's bullet doesn't appear to have broken any bones or hit anything vital. I'm relieved to see that there is an exit wound in my friend's back. I didn't want to have to go digging for a bullet.

I set up a rough camp in the kitchen. There's an old rusted stove there, and I manage to get a fire going with broken bits of wood from the collapsed roof. I heat some water, clean his wound and wrap it up as best I can. I'm relieved to see the bleeding slow down.

When I've got Nah-kee-tats-an settled as comfortably as I can manage, I go outside in the gathering dark to find Coronado waiting patiently. My ribs hurt dreadfully, but I manage to catch a couple of other horses as well and take the bedrolls from them so we have something to sleep on.

The next morning I drag the bodies away. Animals have been at some of them, but I don't have the strength to bury them in the hard ground. I simply pile them into a storeroom that still has a door on it. I find Alfonso Ramirez's scalp by the fireplace where Ed must have dropped it when I charged him. I throw it into the storeroom with the others. Then I ride into town.

I buy us some supplies, food for us and the horses and clean clothes. I must look pretty bad, because people stare and give me a wide berth as I go about my business. It's obvious that I'm in pain from my ribs, but no one offers to help. There is a *medico* in town, but I don't bring him out. I wonder if he'll treat a wounded Apache. He doesn't speak much English, but in my halting Spanish I ask him to put together a bundle of bandages, swabs and ointments.

When I return to the hacienda in the afternoon of the second day, Nah-kee-tats-an is running a fever. He's lying by the stove, wrapped in a bedroll, shivering and sweating. I try to keep him cool and feed him some-thing, but by nightfall he's delirious and speaking loudly in his native tongue. Eventually, toward dawn, he quiets down and I sleep.

I wake up in full daylight with the local medico standing in the doorway staring at Nah-kee-tats-an.

"*Él es enfermo*," he says unnecessarily.

"Yes, he is sick," I reply.

The man bustles forward and crouches over Nah-kee-tats-an. He examines the recent wound and the one from the ambush several days ago, nodding and speaking softly to himself. Occasionally he addresses me with a request. "*Agua caliente, por favor.*" I busy myself with the fire, heating water and cooking some food.

At last the medico stands up. He insists on looking at my injuries and binds a wide strip of cotton tightly round my chest. It helps the pain when I move. He hands me some more of the ointment and instructs me in applying it and changing Nah-kee-tats-an's dressings. Already, my friend seems to be sleeping more easily.

I offer the man some breakfast, and we eat in silence. After we are done, he walks through to the main hall and stands looking at the several large dried bloodstains.

"*¿Dónde están los cadáveres?*" he asks.

I take him to the storeroom and haul open the door. A cloud of large flies rise with a loud buzzing sound.

The medico simply nods. He walks over to where I have tethered the horses I have managed to catch. Coronado is there, as is an unsaddled pony that belongs to Nah-kee-tats-an. I have also caught Ed's large black gelding and two other animals. The other two are nowhere to be seen.

"*¿Estos caballos pertenecen a los cadáveres?*" the medico asks.

I tell him that, apart from Coronado and the pony, these horses *do* belong to the dead men. He asks me if I will give him those horses to sell to pay for the medicine. I say sure and he ties the horses to his wagon and leaves.

The next day, two men with shovels turn up and bury the bodies. They cross themselves a lot as they work and stay well away from me and Nah-kee-tats-an, whose fever has broken and who is taking some food.

On the fifth day the medico returns, examines us both and pronounces himself satisfied with our progress. Nah-kee-tats-an is sitting up. He regards the medico suspiciously but allows him to work on his wounds. The medico gives us some more supplies, a bag of feed for the horses and a small bag of silver coins from the sale of the horses. Outside he turns to me as he prepares to mount his horse.

"*¿Usted conoce esta casa?*" he asks.

I say that I do know this house. "*Es la casa de Ramirez.*"

The medico nods. "*Mala suerte. Es una casa de la muerte.*"

"Yes," I agree. It a place of bad luck and death. On an impulse I ask, "*¿Usted conoce Luis Santiago de Borica?*"

The medico's face brightens into a smile at the mention of Santiago. "*Sí. Sí. Él es un buen hombre.*"

I agree that Santiago is a good man and tell the medico of my evening with him. Then I tell him he is a good man and thank him for his help. "*Gracias por su ayuda.*"

"*No es nada.*" The medico shrugs off my gratitude and mounts. "*Vaya con dios.*"

I wave as he rides out the hacienda gate.

"I will leave in the morning," Nah-kee-tats-an announces as we sit by the stove after our evening meal.

"Are you well enough?" I ask.

Nah-kee-tats-an nods. "And I have lived within walls long enough."

"Where will you go?"

"I will find Victorio and fight with him."

"Your father, Too-ah-yay-say, says there are too many Americans. He thinks you cannot win."

"But that does not mean we should not fight. You and I fought here against the scalp hunters, and now they are dead and we are alive."

I nod agreement. "Why were you here?" I ask the question that's been nagging at me.

"I was trailing the men who scalped my friends. When I saw they were coming here, I climbed in a window at the back and waited."

"I'm very glad you did."

"What will you do, Busca?" Nah-kee-tats-an asks.

I haven't given it much thought. I've been too focused on finding out what happened to my father and on simply surviving. Suddenly I know what I must do. Many people have helped me on my journey by telling me their stories, which have turned out to be parts of my story. I will return the way I came and tell Santiago and Wellington how the story ends. And I will write a letter to my mother in Yale. I won't go back up to British Columbia. Not now. I'm not ready and, if I am honest, this harsh land fascinates me. I feel it is not done with me yet.

"I will tell a story," I reply.

My vague answer seems to satisfy Nah-kee-tats-an.

"Perhaps, one day," he says, "our stories will cross again."

When I wake the next morning, Nah-kee-tats-an is gone.

In no great hurry, I make breakfast, pack up my few belongings, saddle Coronado and leave the blood-stained hacienda behind. I am sad that my father is dead and that I never got to see him again, but I feel relieved that I know. It's as if a huge weight has been lifted from me. I'm free at last.

JOHN WILSON is the author of twenty-nine books for juveniles, teens and adults. His self-described "addiction to history" has resulted in many award-winning novels that bring the past alive for young readers. Wilson spends significant portions of the year traveling across the country speaking in schools, leaving his audiences excited about our past. You can learn more about John, his books and his presentations by visiting his blog: johnwilson_author@blogspot.com.

The following is an excerpt from another
exciting novel by JOHN WILSON.

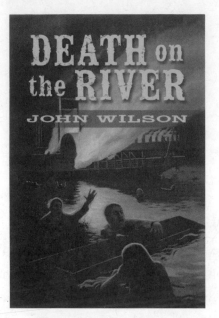

978-1-55469-111-1 $12.95 pb
978-1-55469-257-6 $18.95 hc

CAPTURED AND CONFINED to the
Confederate prison camp at Andersonville
in June 1864, young Jake Clay forms an
unlikely alliance with Billy Sharp, an unscru-
pulous opportunist who teaches him to survive
no matter what the cost. By war's end Jake is
haunted by the ghosts of those who've died so
he could live. Now his fateful journey home will
come closer to killing him than Andersonville
did, but it will also provide him with one last
chance at redemption.

ONE

I pull back the thin blanket and swing my legs over the edge of the bed. When I stand up, the tiled floor feels icy cold on my bare feet, but that's good—it reminds me that I'm alive.

There's a pile of clothes on the table by the bed. They're not mine; they were dropped off by a smiling nun who went round the ward asking if any of us needed anything. I said I wanted clothes and a pair of shoes, and her smile broadened so far that I thought her face would split. The guy in the bed beside me said he wanted his legs back, and she hurried off to help someone else.

I begin to dress, slowly because my hands are still sore. The legless guy turns his head. "Where you going?" he asks.

"Home," I say.

"Where's home?"

"Upstate New York," I answer as I painfully button my pants.

"That's a long way from Memphis."

I nod.

"You walking all that way?" he asks.

"Expect so."

"Lucky bastard," he says.

I pull on the shoes the nun brought. They're a surprisingly good fit.

"City shoes," the man says. "Won't last long on the road."

"I'll worry about that when I have to."

I shake his hand. It hurts, but then I'm used to pain.

"Think about me when you get blisters," he says with a bitter laugh.

"I will." I smile back.

I plan to walk north until I get home. It's not much of a plan. I've got some money, my discharge pay and a piece of paper that says that Jake Clay is no longer needed by the Union army. I'll scrounge or buy what food I can and sleep rough when I have to.

Walking all that way is a strange thing to do, but it's perfect for me. I want to go home, but I'm scared of getting there. Walking is slow enough that I can feel I'm going home but still postponing the arrival to the distant future.

At least I won't be alone.

The War between the States has been over for only two months, and the roads and rivers are clogged with men traveling in all directions. Most of them will make it home one way or another. That's the easy part. It's what you bring home inside your head that's the problem.

My hope is that the long walk will give me a chance to sort out what is going on in *my* head. Walking has always calmed me, helped me see things rationally. Maybe the miles and the dust will wear off the past I carry like a weight on my back. Make me forget the twelve months since I first went into battle that hopeless, bloody day at Cold Harbor. Make me forget the things I have seen, the things I have done, the ghosts who haunt my dreams. I can never go back to being the naïve kid I was before then, but with luck I can move forward.

I hope, but I don't know. Perhaps it's not possible to forget that you've been to Hell.

 # TWO

in this to my back and I'll do the same fer you."

I don't know the name of the man standing beside me in the shallow trench. I've only been a part of Baldy Smith's XVIII Corps for a few days. I arrived just in time to move up the James River to these crossroads at Cold Harbor.

"What is it?" I ask, looking at the sheet of paper he's holding.

"You're one of them new fellas that joined just afore we come up here?"

I nod.

"Ever bin in a fight?"

I shake my head.

"Well, I've bin in plenty," the man says. He's missing one of his front teeth, which causes his voice to whistle slightly as he speaks. "And this's the way it is. Soldier al'ays knows afore a battle if'n he'll be on the winnin' or the losin' side.

"Now, bein' on the winnin' side don't mean that you ain't gonna get kilt or have yer leg blowed off, but bein' on the losin' side makes it more likely, and we're sure as hell on the losin' side this day."

"How do you know?" I ask in shock. I had assumed the attack we had prepared for all yesterday would win us the battle.

The man gives me a look of pity. "What'd we do all yesterday?" he asks.

"We dug these trenches," I say.

"And disturbed the bones of a good few of the boys who fought here two years back at Gaines Mill," he says. "That weren't good luck. Where're the Rebs?"

I point through the trees into the thick dawn fog.

The man nods. "And what d'you think they was doin' yesterday?"

"Digging?"

"That'd be right. Diggin' like their lives depend on it, 'cause they surely do. Now, me and a few of the boys went forrard yesterday evenin' and saw them diggin's.

They got log breastworks zigzaggin' all over hell's half acre with cannons pointin' through them every few yards.

"In a couple of minutes, we're goin' over there, and as soon as we walk out of that fog, them breastworks is gonna light up like a Fourth of July picnic and there ain't gonna be space fer a mosquito 'tween them Minnie balls and canister shot. That's why we're on a hidin' to nothin' in this fight.

"Now, I plan to die facing the enemy, and I want my folks to know what happened to me. So you pin this paper with my name on it to the back of my jacket so's they'll know whose corpse it is after the fight, and I'll do the same fer you."

I feel like an undertaker, pinning the paper to his back. I notice his name: Zach Moore, written in a childlike hand.

Zach tears a page out of his diary for me to write my name on. I notice the last entry in the same scrawl: *June 3, 1864. Today I was kilt.*

For the first time I feel real fear. Not nervousness, worry or a vague sense of dread, but cold, specific, gut-wrenching terror. I can almost feel the lead balls ripping their way through my stomach and chest, shattering bones and turning vital organs to mush.

I begin to breathe rapidly and hold on to the dirt wall of the earthworks to stop from falling over.

Zach spins me around and slaps me hard across the cheek. The pain brings tears to my eyes but it gives me a focus. Gradually, my breathing calms.

"No point in becomin' a shiverin' coward," Zach says. "If'n yer time's up today, ain't nothin' you can do 'bout it. Now come on, let's get this thing done."

Zach and I clamber out of the trench and form up with the rest of the division. I feel better with others around me, especially Zach. I've only known him a few minutes, yet he already feels like a brother. I have the stupid idea that if I stay close to him, I'll be all right.

We walk forward through the trees. The sharp smell of wood smoke from a thousand campfires catches my nose. It's a comforting smell, reminding me of fishing trips back home.

The division is moving forward in grim silence, only the rattle of equipment and the occasional shouted order or curse reaching me.

We walk out of the trees, but I still cannot see the enemy fortifications through the fog. Off to my left, a roll of musket fire sounds like the clack of Mother's new Willcox and Gibbs pedal sewing machine. Then we are in the open. A flat field stretches away to another line of trees, along the edge of which the Rebels have dug in.

Zach's right—the breastworks do indeed look formidable. Rebel flags hang limp above the solid wood and earth walls, but behind them is a hive of activity. A forest of muskets, with long bayonets glinting in the rising sun, points at us, and the black muzzles of cannon are being pushed forward.

"Come on, boys," the officer in front of me shouts as he raises his sword and breaks into a rapid trot. Almost immediately, the breastworks explode in a solid wall of fire. The roar reaches me a split second later, but above it I can hear the whine of Minnie balls. Large gaps appear in our formation where canister shot from the cannons rips men to shreds. The battlefield disappears in a rolling wall of thick gray smoke.

The enemy cannot possibly see us through the smoke their cannons and muskets are throwing out, but it doesn't matter; as long as they keep on firing, they cannot miss. We hurry forward, many men hunching over as if pushing against a strong wind.

The crack of the muskets and the roar of the cannons are irregular now but still constant. We have been told not to fire our muskets until we are almost at the breastworks. Good advice, if any of us make the breastworks.

Men are falling all around. It's not as theatrical as I imagined in my childhood games. Men in battle don't usually throw their arms up, pirouette dramatically and throw themselves to the ground. Usually it's just a grunt, a sagging to the knees and an almost apologetic collapse.

Everything around me seems incredibly vivid and real. Every sight I see is sharp and every noise and smell the strongest I have ever experienced. I see a man's arm fly off and spiral slowly through the air in a red spray. I hear the soft thud of lead balls hitting the flesh of the man in front of me. I smell his blood.

I feel Zach grip my arm. I turn to see him smiling at me. A small tear in his shirt is already seeping blood. Before I can decide what to do, there is a dull cracking sound. Zach's head jerks back, his cap flies off and a small dark hole appears in his forehead. The smile is replaced by a puzzled expression, his grip loosens and he slips sideways.

"Zach?" I say stupidly as I crouch over him. He's already dead, lying on his back with blood covering half his face and his shirt front. I roll him over so that someone will see the paper on his back.

"You there. Get on."

I look up to see the officer standing over me. He's

still holding his sword in the air, but the blade is just a stump, shattered by a Minnie ball. He's not a lot older than me, but he's trying to look older by growing a mustache. It's not working; his hair is fair and his mustache looks like the fuzz on a peach. Before I have a chance to reply, the officer groans quietly and sits down.

Strangely, I don't try to help him. He has ordered me on, and that's what I do. I get up and keep going forward. I'm in a daze. I can still see and hear what is happening around me, but it's happening to someone else. I don't even care that Zach's dead.

My cap is torn away, and I feel a Minnie ball tug at my trousers. The smoke swirls and I see the Rebel lines. They are surprisingly close. I can see enemy soldiers clambering on top of them to get a better shot at us. I swing my musket around, cock it and aim at a large bearded man slightly to my right. I pull the trigger and he disappears in a cloud of smoke. I wonder if I hit him.

I rush forward and begin to scramble up the breastworks. The wood is sticky with sap, and green shoots still grow out of the fresh-cut timber. There's a man on top and he lunges down at me with his bayonet. I knock it aside and stab him in the thigh. He yells in pain and falls backward.

I only see the musket butt as a dark shape out of the corner of my eye. It catches me on the right temple. I hear a loud crack and hope it's not my skull breaking. There is a sense of falling backward into space, and then everything goes black.